BEYOND THE BURNING TIME

BEYOND THE BURNING TIME

KATHRYN LASKY

THE BLUE SKY PRESS

An Imprint of Scholastic Inc.

The Blue Sky Press

For information regarding permission, please write to:
Permissions Department, The Blue Sky Press,
an imprint of Scholastic Inc.,
555 Broadway, New York, New York 10012

The Blue Sky Press is a trademark of Scholastic Inc.

Library of Congress Cataloging-in-Publication Data

Lasky, Kathryn
Beyond the burning time / Kathryn Lasky
p.   cm.
Summary: When, in the winter of 1692, accusations
of witchcraft surface in her small New England village,
twelve-year-old Mary Chase fights
to save her mother from execution.
ISBN 0-590-47331-X
1. Trials (Witchcraft) — Massachusetts — Salem —
Juvenile fiction.
[1. Trials (Witchcraft) — Fiction.   2. Witchcraft — Fiction.
3. Salem (Mass.) — History — Colonial period, ca. 1600–1775 —
Fiction.]
I. Title.
PZ7.L3274Bc   1994
[Fic] — dc20   94-5231
                                                        CIP
                                                        AC

12 11 10 9 8 7 6 5 4 3 2 1   4 5 6 7 8 9/9

Designed by Elizabeth B. Parisi
Printed in the United States of America   37
First printing, October 19, 1994

SALEM 1692

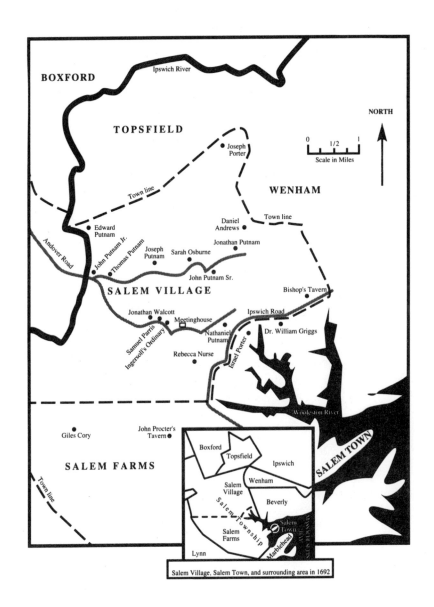

Salem Village, Salem Town, and surrounding area in 1692

BEYOND THE
BURNING TIME

CHAPTER
ONE

It was winter light, hard and metallic. The setting sun held no warmth these January days. The girl pulled her cloak tighter, hunched her shoulders, and shrank back into her hood. Salem Town and the raw chill of the wind from the sea were behind her, and with each step the smell of kelp became fainter. Yet she felt colder. It made no sense.

It would be dark soon, and she knew she must not linger. She still had the better part of a mile to go until she met up with the Ipswich Road, and then another two miles to her house.

She was following the river, and at this point it began to narrow until it was just a creek. The thick gloom of the forest around her obscured the gray twilight, and soon the babble of the creek was muffled. All she could hear through the deep shadows of the snowy woods was the moaning and creaking of trees in a gnawing wind.

Mary Chase now concentrated on each step. It was a game she had invented to push away the thoughts that had been pressing upon her these past several days since the strangeness had begun. She

1

walked carefully, making a pattern in the snow with her heavy boots. If she stepped a certain way, she could make a print very similar to a rabbit's winter track. If she stepped just right, then squinted just so in the dwindling light, then hummed a tune, she could fill her mind and get past the darkest part of the woods. That was where the Tall Man with his iron-clasped book was said to be. Mary shivered. But her fear of the Tall Man and his book was nothing compared to this. This strangeness.

"Oh, stop it, Mary!" she shouted. She stomped her foot in the snow, ruining the print. Then she clapped her hand over her mouth. The hood of her cloak fell back. She couldn't believe it! She had actually spoken aloud to herself. Soon people would be likening her to Sarah Good, who was touched in the head.

She looked straight ahead, to where the path joined the Ipswich Road. In a gap between the trees, the sinking sun became suddenly lurid. Its amber light swirled like an egg yolk, streaking the sky with scarlet.

Mary felt a funny turn in her stomach. It was an egg yolk, they said, that Tituba had swirled in the water to tell the girls' fortunes. And that was where the strangeness had begun, in the kitchen of Tituba, the slave of the Reverend Samuel Parris in the Village of Salem.

*　*　*

It had all started with fortune-telling. Several girls had begun to go to Tituba's kitchen to find out about whom they might marry and such. It wasn't right, of course, because fortune-telling was a "little sorcery," and one must not try to sound out the mysteries of God. But these little sorceries were tempting; the future was so uncertain. The threat of Indians was constant, and disease could wipe out half a village in a matter of weeks.

Mary Chase was sure that in many of the houses along the Ipswich Road and beyond, sieves, scissors, and candles were kept for divining such things. She herself was tempted to go when Mercy Lewis had told her what went on in Tituba's kitchen. But Mary Chase didn't care about finding out who her husband might be. No, she would prefer to know if the barley they had planted in the new field would come up this spring. And if Nathaniel Ingersoll had been right when he said that the barley was a good "field starter," making the soil "tractable" for corn to be planted in the following years. And she also wanted to know if the cow they had bought eighteen months before was really going to be barren. If so, that would be a problem — and how did one go about selling a barren cow?

But she hadn't gone to Tituba's kitchen when Mercy Lewis had invited her. She didn't live as close to the Reverend Parris's parsonage as the other girls. The Parris's nine-year-old daughter Betty, her eleven-year-old cousin Abigail, and three older girls were going to Tituba's kitchen; Susannah Sheldon and Elizabeth Booth were both eighteen, and Mary Walcott would soon be seventeen.

The circle of these girls continued to widen. Mercy Lewis had gone and brought twelve-year-old Ann Putnam, who was the same age as Mary. Then Mary Warren and Sarah Churchill, who were both almost twenty, joined.

Of course, nobody knew anything about the circle and the fortune-telling for a long time, until the fits started. Why, it had been early December when Mercy Lewis had first asked Mary to join. And although people might have known that the girls spent time at the Parris's, no one would suspect little sorceries, for it was, after all, the parsonage.

Then Betty Parris got sick. At first, they said it was just forgetfulness. She would skip an errand or forget a chore. But her behavior was odd. As Goodwife Dawson described it, her eyes looked as if transfixed, and during these spells, Betty Parris could not even hear when spoken to.

Within days, the sickness began in the others. After Betty, it came upon her cousin Abigail, twisting the child into such postures that her aunt was said to have run from the house screaming that the child would snap her neck. Then, one by one, it overcame the rest of the circle. It was hard for Mary

Chase to imagine. And she did not want to. She stomped ahead now through the snow.

The violent colors had paled as the sun seeped behind the horizon. The sky was darkening fast. Mary turned on to the Ipswich Road. She must hurry home. She must tell her mother how well her brother Caleb was doing.

It had been wonderful to visit him today in the Salem shipyard, where he was an apprentice. He was working with the master carpenter himself on scarfing the stem for the new ship, a brigantine to go into the trade. Soon it would take cargoes of grain and cod, mackerel and fur to the West Indies, the Canaries, Newfoundland, and London. Ah, to be a boy! How exciting to be making a piece of a ship that would sail in a distant sea!

Mary's mother would be so proud of Caleb. When Mary's father died, her mother insisted that Caleb not forsake his apprenticeship. It was too important. She and Mary could manage the farm with some hired help. For this had been Mary's father's dream: to build a link with the sea and the expanding trade of the ports of Salem and Boston. Caleb was the hope.

Oh, yes, Mary's father had had wonderful dreams — dreams of ships with holds filled with the grain they would grow and salt pork they would make on their own land to trade in far-off places.

But Mary's father had died suddenly two winters

before. He had caught a chill that turned into a raging fever. He was gone before the doctor could even bleed him.

The dream had not been fulfilled. Fortunately, the mortgage on the farm had been paid off just a month before Mary's father had died. Through hard work, careful planning, and a good harvest, Virginia Chase had managed to purchase another few acres of land, which she knew were just itching to grow corn and barley. Barley first, her friend Nathaniel Ingersoll had told her. That was best for the soil, and the soil would be best for the barley — then the corn.

Soon it would be completely dark. Mary preferred the darkness to this gathering gloom; long shadows of winter trees lurched across the snow, their skeletal limbs jerking in the fitful wind.

Suddenly, out of the near darkness, a figure appeared. It seemed to have melted out of thin air, hunched and scurrying.

Oh, no! Mary heard the sound of muttering on the shifted wind.

It had to be Sarah Good, the woman everyone said was touched. Who else would be out in such a flimsy wrap, not even a cloak? It appeared that she was wearing just a torn old quilt drawn up between her legs and flung across her shoulders. Her dress ballooned out round her stockinged calves like pantaloons. Her pipe was jammed between her teeth, and Mary could even see the glow of the ember in its bowl.

The woman was heading right toward her. Mary hoped Sarah Good would not stop to beg. She was glad that she had already delivered the ham hock and four-grain cake to Caleb.

They both slowed as they were about to pass. But Sarah Good did not stop. She just turned in the odd way she had and stared at Mary while she walked. She was a most haggish-looking old thing, but then Mary gulped in surprise. Was that a big, round bulge under that filthy quilt? She must be carrying something she had begged, certainly not a baby. Sarah Good was much too old to be having babies.

Mary raced on, averting her eyes. She wanted to take a second look at that bulge, but her house was just another quarter mile down the road. And now she really was cold, and eager for home and the warmth it promised.

CHAPTER
TWO

In the dark outer room beside the scullery, Mary took off her heavy boots and began rubbing her toes. Her clogs were set by the door, and Gilly's boots were propped against the wall. Now why would Gilly leave his heavy boots here, and walk the long distance home without them? This hired man was indeed simple.

Her mother said Gilly did this kind of thing because he treasured Mary's father's boots so much, he was afraid something might happen to them. So he only wore them when he was working at the Chases' farm. Before Jacob Chase died, Gilly had helped out on occasion. Now Gilly came almost every day.

Well, Mary's feet were fiercely cold, and she wasn't going to worry about Gilly and his simple ways. She rubbed her toes harder, put the clogs on, and walked into the buttery. The churn stood rinsed and upside down. The plain shapes of butter blocks and headcheese wrapped in cloth were set on a table. Mary could hear another voice beyond the buttery door that led into the house. Her mother must have a visitor.

"I did indeed!" the voice crackled. "I went right over and straightened out her limbs — first her arm. It was twisted in a position you'd never believe possible. All crook'd up behind her back, tight as anything."

Mary stood in the shadows. It was Goody Dawson. Goodwife Dawson was a plump little woman whose face always reminded Mary of a potato: smooth and slightly yellowish with a few darker pinpoint-sized speckles. Her mouth was very tiny and was a bit lost, tucked between her rounded cheeks and chin; it hardly seemed to move when she spoke. Her words had no visible origin; they just floated out of the puffy contours of her face.

Today, however, Mary stood transfixed. Goody Dawson's words painted a vivid picture of a terrible seizure. But whose seizure was it? It sounded as if a new girl had been afflicted.

Mary's mother and the woman stood in a pool of light that radiated from the immense fireplace. Their long shadows slid up toward the ceiling. Goodwife Dawson was now jerking her own arms around as she described her efforts to straighten the afflicted girl's limbs. The antic shadows of her arms danced a crazy jig on the heavy beams. "I really never saw anything to the like . . . frothing at the mouth, she was. And her eyes rolled back so far in her head, I thought they'd turn round completely and come up from the bottom."

Mary saw her mother wince at this detail. It was not the first time Mary had heard this plump woman rattle on, delighting in giving a flourish here or there to a tale, as if spicing up a plain gruel. Goody Dawson savored such detail.

Mary found the woman more irritating than usual. And she wouldn't for one second believe that eyeballs could turn complete spins in their eye sockets.

"That would be near impossible, wouldn't it?" Mary asked, stepping out of the door alcove and into the main room of the house.

"Mary!" Virginia Chase looked up. "My goodness, child, announce yourself. I had no idea you had returned." Mary's mother's face looked tense and slightly flushed, but she seemed pleased that Mary had come in at just this moment — as if she herself had had enough of Goodwife Dawson's recitation.

"But Goody Dawson — of whom are you speaking?"

"Young Ann Putnam. She fell down day before yesterday for the first time. Now, three more times she has been afflicted. I heard the fracas this morning when I was passing by, taking some eggs over to Goody Brown — all her hens stopped laying, just like that." She flicked a plump hand in the air, paused, and looked darkly at Virginia.

"You say young Ann Putnam?" Mary asked.

"Yes, and fits like you've never seen."

"I've never seen any," Mary said.

"Oh, her eyes rolled back, and her neck twisted . . ." Goody Dawson was off again.

Virginia bent over and picked up a spindle of unwound yarn from her workbox and set it on the swift. Furiously she began winding the hank of yarn into a ball. She shook her head and pursed her lips. A vertical line on either side of her mouth suddenly creased her face. The lines always appeared when Virginia Chase was in the grip of fear or worry.

"They have always been very high strung, the Putnam women, particularly Ann senior," Virginia said softly.

"Well, yes, yes," Goody Dawson nodded. "So many babies both she and her sister lost. But of course it's young Ann who is having the fits, not her mother."

"Nonetheless, it is young Ann who is taken by her mother to the cemetery nearly every day to cry at those babies' graves. It is not fit . . ." Virginia hesitated. She set down the growing ball of yarn and looked off at the ceiling beams in the front of the room. Then she clamped her eyes shut. "It is not meet and proper, not healthy to suckle a child on such sadness . . . such bitterness."

"You're right, Virginia. You're right. It's a pity.

The child has always been frail, with a terrible pallor." Goodwife Dawson sighed, the comfortable kind of sigh that seemed to befit stout, well-padded women of certain years. "Well, nothing we can do about it. I'm just glad I was there and could be of some help." The words poked the air, and a look of complete satisfaction spread across the potato face. "Ah, I hear my husband's cart coming now. I'll be on my way."

Virginia led her to the door. As soon as she shut the door, she walked back to her chair by the hearth and sank heavily into it. Mary looked at her closely. Her mother suddenly appeared old, as old as she had on the day Mary's father had died.

Virginia pressed her fingers into her forehead and ran them up to the edge of her muslin cap. It was as if she were trying to knit together the thoughts in her head. She must have felt Mary studying her, for she opened her eyes wide and smiled. But it wasn't a real smile. It was forced.

"So tell me, dear, how is our Caleb?"

"Oh, wonderful, Mother. Would you believe that he is working with the master on the scarfing of the brig *Ezra Shattuck?*"

"You mean just the two of them — our Caleb and Master Jeremy?" Her eyes widened now in genuine delight. "Oh, your father would be so proud!" Her face relaxed. "Now, dear, why don't you get the Bible?"

Mary fetched the Bible from the shelf. A dark ribbon marked the verses they had read in the meetinghouse on the previous Sunday: Revelation, chapter 12. She scanned the verses silently:

And there was war in heaven: Michael and his angels fought against the dragon; and the dragon fought his angels . . .
And prevailed not. . . .
And the great dragon was cast out, that old serpent, called the Devil, and Satan, which deceiveth the whole world. . . .
No man might buy or sell, save he that had the mark, or the name of the beast . . .

The Reverend Parris drew heavily on Revelation for his text each Sunday, and Mary knew that her mother would appreciate something more soothing this evening. So she turned to one of Virginia's favorite psalms and began to read:

"He appointed the moon for seasons: the sun knoweth his going down.
"Thou makest darkness, and it is night:
wherein all the beasts of the forest do creep forth.
"The young lions roar after their prey, and seek their meat from God.
"The sun ariseth, they gather themselves together, and lay them down in their dens. . . ."

13

Mary continued reading. Her mother leaned her head back against the rest on the chair and closed her eyes.

"Oh Lord, how manifold are thy works!"

Mary read on. She was getting to the part her mother loved best, the part about the wide sea and the creeping beasts, both large and small, and the ships! But suddenly Virginia jerked her head forward, and her eyes opened wide with unmistakable fear.

"Mary!" Virginia's voice was sharp, as if she were about to scold.

"What is it, Mother?"

"Does anybody know, aside from myself and your brother, that I have taught you to read?"

"Uh. . . ." Mary was at a loss. She did not really remember if she had ever mentioned it before or had occasion where people might see her reading. "I . . . I can't say. . . . I really doubt it."

"Well," said Virginia, leaning forward, "it's better you not mention it." Her mother spoke tersely. "Here, let me read tonight for a change, anyway." Virginia Chase reached for the Bible.

Mary could not understand. She had thought her mother had always been pleased by her ability to read. In meeting on Sunday, many of the men could read, but it was most unusual for women, let alone girls. One did not need to read in meeting; for the most part, the texts were etched in the memory. There were no schools in Salem Village. Boys often

14

learned to read as part of an apprenticeship, but girls rarely did. Would she never be able to read aloud again?

Her mother began another psalm, and although the words were beautiful and spoke of rivers and streams and the glad city of God, it was not the same. Despite the music of the psalms, a sense of dread was seeping into the room. It climbed into the ceiling beams and gathered with the shadows in the dark corners. It waited — silent and unspoken. But it was there, and it was felt.

They blew out the candles before going to bed, and Mary was trimming the mantles in the oil lamps when she suddenly remembered Sarah Good.

"Mother," she said, turning from the table on which the lamps stood by the huge hearth. The fire was now dying down. "I saw Sarah Good on the Ipswich Road this night, and she looked wilder than ever."

"Oh, the poor thing. Yes, I know. She was here today and left just before Goody Dawson arrived, thank heavens!" Goodwife Dawson was not one for much patience with the likes of Sarah Good. "I gave her a smoked hock and some four-grain cake, and a bit of molasses."

"Molasses!"

"Yes, I know it's dear, but the poor old thing, well . . . she's to have another one."

"A baby! Mother! That's impossible. She's so old."

"Not too old." Virginia sighed wearily. "She looks older than she is. Little Dorcas is only four or five."

"Sarah Good looks seventy if a day."

"Well, she is not. She has just had a hard life."

"If she didn't behave so strangely all the time and smoke that pipe, perhaps — "

But Virginia cut her off. "Be charitable, Mary. Her pipe and her muttering have no more to do with the person inside Sarah than does the color of your hair or your eyes, or the way you raise that minnow of a golden eyebrow of yours when you speak as archly as you do now." She smiled broadly, came up behind her daughter, and embraced her. They stood for a moment in the light of the fire's embers, then went upstairs to their bedrooms.

Long after she had said her prayers, Mary could see the glow of the lamplight from her mother's room and the edge of her mother's kneeling shadow. The prayers were taking longer tonight. What was she praying for? Did one dare to listen to another's prayers? Was she praying away the dread? Or searching in her prayers for hope? But her mother was always full of hope. How else could she have bought the field and bravely planted barley with the hope for corn? And she had hope for her children — that is why Caleb was right now scarfing the stem on the brig *Ezra Shattuck,* and why Mary Chase was probably the only girl in all of Salem Village who could read, and had been since she was five. It was because her mother had hope and faith, and belief in God and her children. There was no room for dread here.

Mary's eyes had become used to the darkness. The dark shapes were familiar. She liked the cozy geometry of the room at night — the corners that met under the low, sloping roofline, the dormer just across from her bed with its leaded glass. The moon, although not full, was riding high now, and its reflection on the snow tossed a silver path of light through the small window.

The moon path ended at her bureau and illuminated a box that sat on top. It was the dovetailed box made by Caleb during the first year of his apprenticeship. It was small, and that was part of its beauty; it was complicated, but it looked simple. And if one looked at it very carefully, one could see that not only were the dovetails perfectly cut, but the grain of the ends of the dovetails flowed as seamlessly into the face of the box as water in a stream joining a river.

Master Jeremy had said it was the best box any apprentice had ever made in his shop. And Caleb had given it to Mary. This perfect object was hers to keep. There was only one thing she wanted more. And that was to be able to make such a box herself. She envied her brother. It was wrong to envy. She knew it was wrong, but nonetheless she did it anyway. No matter how hard she prayed, the envy would not go away.

Despite the cold, she got up now from her bed and walked across the floor in her bare feet. Sometimes she just needed to touch the box, to run her fingers over the beautiful dovetails. It was hard for her to believe that it was an inanimate object. The oiled finish had a life to it. She knew the grain so well, she thought she could feel it even though it had been sanded smooth.

She kneeled down now and placed the box on the floor in the middle of the moonlit stream that poured through her window. The flair of the dovetails, the way they interlocked with the pins, the true craftsmanship, never ceased to amaze Mary. But it was something more simple than the artistry that beckoned and intrigued her. It was the skill itself, the craft of joinery. She wanted to learn that. To be able to join things, to make them strong. To make things that were able to hold and to weather well.

The box held some seeds she had gathered at the end of summer from a patch of lupine that grew near the shore. Caleb was now working on a ship that would carry cargo across storm-laced seas to places with faraway names. There was something very fine about that, very noble and good, as good as being a minister or a doctor. Yes indeed, she would rather be a master carpenter than a king.

She put the box back on the bureau and walked to the window. The snowy field stretched blue under the moonlight.

Mary knew she should be asleep, for she must get up early to help Gilly with the milking. But she liked to stand by the window, stretching her imagination across the fields to the shore, to the sea, and then beyond. Most people were asleep at this hour, except possibly down the road at John Procter's tavern, where wayfarers were permitted to buy cider and beer and liquor. Goodman Procter's license specified that he could sell only to strangers — outsiders who would frequent this route on their way to other places. On this particular night, however, not everyone was asleep; and even given Goodwife Dawson's descriptions, Mary could not have imagined the terrible scene occurring at that very moment in the parsonage.

The Reverend Parris had just finished the nighttime prayers when his eleven-year-old niece Abigail fell to the floor and began barking like a dog. She then rushed toward the fireplace and tried to crawl directly into it. And she would have done so if Tituba's husband had not pulled her away. She then grabbed a log and flung it across the room.

"Who does this? Who does this to you?" the Reverend Parris was shouting at the top of his voice.

As she stood at her window, dreaming of the sea

and sailing ships, Mary Chase never could have imagined Abigail's contorted and stiffened limbs, the horror in all the faces in that room.

And was there a mirror hanging darkly in the night? For not far from the Parris household, but a mile or more from the Chases', Ann Putnam senior stood at a nearly identical dormer window. Except for the distance between Mary Chase and Goodwife Putnam, the figures could have been gazing directly at one another. But these were no mirror images.

Mary stood calm and still, loving the moonlight on the snow, wishing for an owl's soft *whooo whooo* in the night, and imagining the land unfolding to the east and the world beyond. She had resolved to try to make a box of her own in fine-grained wood with dovetailed joints, and she dreamed of someday building a small boat with her brother, a fine little skiff with seakindly lines that they could sail in the river.

Goodwife Putnam, however, stood trembling in front of her window. She did not see the snow, or the moon. Her mind was lit with blood-tinged images from the Book of Revelation that she and young Ann pored over nightly. Her husband now called to her from the feather bed to come to sleep. But Goodwife Putnam stayed in front of the window, her mind's eye looking for her dead babies in the sky.

A star twinkled over the apple orchard, a very bright one. She wondered if that was the star in the Bible passage, the star where *'they shall hunger no more, neither thirst anymore; neither shall the sun light on them, nor any heat.'* Was that where her babies were, on that star?

CHAPTER
THREE

Sometimes Mary thought she could hear his boots crunching in the snow half a mile down the road. She could always hear the creak of the hinge on the gate when Gilly came through, and by that time she had to be downstairs pulling on her mud boots. It was hard these dark winter mornings when it was still cold enough to make things break. The worst part was the distance between the warmth of the bed and the barn.

The cold ambushed her as she stepped from the bed. She leaned against the chimney wall while she dressed; it was the warmest place in the room, but the chimney was cold now. The new fire had not yet penetrated its stone. Sometimes her teeth chattered so hard and her hands were so shaky, she could barely pull on her stockings. This was the hardest part. She had heard about how it sometimes got so cold an iron anvil could crack, and if iron could break, certainly the cold this morning could shatter her bones.

Once she was in the barn, she was fine. For although you could still see your breath, the animals radiated heat. The piles of manure were steaming on the floor, and a warm wash of air from the animals' breathing seemed to swirl through the barn. Altogether there were six cows, a half dozen sheep, eighteen chickens, and three pigs.

While she milked the first cow, she pressed her cheek against its warm flank, and the heat of the udder in her hands warmed her clear to her shoulders. She could hear the rumble and gurgle of the cow's guts. Two of the cows would be calving in another few weeks, and then it would soon be lambing time, and finally the piglets would start coming. With these births it meant the death of winter.

Now she heard the gate creak, then thumps in the mud room while Gilly changed his boots. A slice of cold air entered when he opened the barn door.

"Ah, there you are!" He held aloft a lantern. A small pool of pale yellow light encircled his bent figure. If Goody Dawson's face reminded Mary of a potato, Gilly's was a dried apple. Round and crinkled, it seemed to have folded in on itself. He had no teeth, and his mouth seemed to have sunk in somewhere between a chin that swooped up and a nose that hooked down.

Gilly had a low forehead that made his brow slam right into his eyes — but he had only one eye. It was bright as a polished bead, and where the other should have been, there was a slight depression, wrinkled and puckered like an ill-sewn seam. Mary had gradually gotten used to it, but every now and then when Gilly fixed her with that single eye, it seemed to be the other that was really watching her with its perpetual squint. Mary would feel something inside of her flinch, and it felt as if her whole being squinted back at him in some kind of odd, sympathetic reaction.

"Did you hear?"

"Hear what, Gilly?"

"More fits — Abigail Williams nearly set the house on fire. They're going to call for Dr. Griggs." Gilly had fetched another milking stool, and now he set it down by the cow directly behind Mary. His sing-song voice droned on. "But that won't help, I tell you."

Gilly paused, waiting for Mary to ask why it wouldn't help. But she didn't care for the discussion. She had been warm and drowsy and rocked by the rhythms of the milking before Gilly had come in with his talk. It had just been Mary, happily alone with the cow, and the comforting gurgles in the cow's gut, and the splash of the milk in the pail, but now . . . .

"No, it won't help, I tell you . . . because the problem is not in their bodies; it's in the air. They're in the air. You can't catch them, bleed them, put a plaster on them — no, no. It's not like gout, or the fever. They'll be calling Dr. Griggs, I hear say, but . . . ." On and on Gilly went, looping back, repeating what he had already said. Mary stopped listening.

When milking was done, and the pigs were slopped and the stalls cleaned, Mary and Gilly went in for breakfast. Mary had brought a pan of milk for their bread, and Virginia brought out a platter of potatoes fried in salt pork and a bowl of porridge.

Gilly wouldn't say much in front of Virginia Chase. He was mindful not to let his tongue run on when he was around her. Gilly knew he was simple, and he knew Goodwife Chase would never make fun of him like some, but he lived in powerful dread of the words coming out wrong, of saying something foolish in front of her. He never, ever wanted to look a fool in front of Goodwife Virginia Chase. She and her husband Jacob, poor Jacob, were the smartest people he'd ever known. Whenever he put on poor dead Jacob's boots, he even felt himself grow a little bit smarter. No, he mustn't look a fool. It would be disrespectful. Why, she might even take away the boots. So he sat at the table quietly and dunked his bread in the still-warm milk and thought about nothing.

Mary looked at Gilly out of the corner of her eye. The tip of his long, curving nose nearly met his chin to make a complete circle. He pushed the chunks of sopping bread in the small sunken hole that was his mouth. Sometimes a drop of milk clung to the end of his nose. When he remembered, he used a spoon for his porridge, but more often than not he would just pick up the bowl and slurp it. He had a pattern to the way he ate. It never varied. Three dunks of bread, two slurps of porridge, then three more dunks. At the end there was supposed to be one piece of bread left to mop up the last bit of porridge. Usually there was. But sometimes, if he hadn't gauged it right, he would be left with too much bread and not enough porridge, or too much porridge and not a last piece of bread. Then he would stare into the bowl and grunt, and he would be in a bad humor for the next quarter of an hour. But none of Gilly's moods lasted too long. He forgot easily. This morning the bread and the porridge came out right. He got up quickly from the table. He was going out to begin mending fences, and he would split another cord of wood.

Mary had just come up from the root cellar with a basket of potatoes and had begun peeling them when her mother appeared and leaned in from the pantry door holding a harness. She had a warm smile on her face and held up a halter.

"What do you say to catching Sass for us?"

"You don't mean it, Mother!"

"I do indeed. Plowing time is just round the corner, and Sass — you know how ornery she gets if we don't get her into the harness a few times before."

Indeed Mary did know, but this was one of her favorite things to do — take Sass out for a bit of a run. "Where will we go?"

"I thought I'd bring Rebecca Nurse a four-grain cake. She's been ailing the past few weeks."

"Really?" A frown crinkled Mary's brow. Rebecca Nurse was one of her favorite people. Mary had no grandparents living, but if she had, she would have wanted a grandmother just like Rebecca Nurse. She was big and soft and had a deep purr of a voice, but there was a quickness to her as well. Her eyes were bright as stones in a gurgling creek. And she was always ready with a quip.

"Oh, we must go by all means, Mother. I wish I could think of something to bring her." Mary paused and then remembered the dovetailed box upstairs with the seeds. "Oh, I know. I'll bring her some of the lupine seeds I gathered over in Salem Town last summer."

"That will be lovely. Rebecca is such a good gardener. Those seeds will do fine inland with her. But first we must go into the village. I have a few errands."

Mary ran upstairs, folded a few seeds into a handkerchief, and tucked it into the cuff of her sleeve. She liked the idea of carrying this promise of blossoms to an old lady in the middle of winter.

CHAPTER
FOUR

Was it the way knots of people stood on the corners in tight, dark groups, or the way a curtain moved, and a face peered round its edge through a pane of leaded glass?

As soon as they drew into the village center, Mary felt that something was wrong. She steered Sass to a hitching post in front of Nathaniel Ingersoll's Ordinary. In the back of the wagon was a large side of salt-cured beef, which Virginia planned to trade for some nails and hinges.

"Don't trouble yourself, Goody Chase. John Indian is here. He'll haul that in for us," Nathaniel Ingersoll said as he came out the tavern door. He seemed especially grim and tight-lipped this morning.

John Indian appeared from around the corner of the house to help. He was a short, stout black man. His wife was Tituba. And this morning he looked as if he were about to buckle under a weight so heavy as not to be imaginable. But he picked up the side of beef and added it to his burden as if it were nothing.

When he disappeared again, Nathaniel Ingersoll turned to Virginia. In a low voice he began, "It's their Betty and Abigail." He nodded toward the parson's house across the road. "They took to fits again last night. John Indian had to drag Abigail from the fire. She had crawled right in, trying to grab burning sticks."

"Oh, mercy!" gasped Virginia.

"Dr. Griggs came today. He examined them and says it's the evil hand."

"What nonsense!"

"Yes, but Goodwife Chase, listen." Ingersoll dropped his voice even lower and stepped closer to both Mary and her mother. "Say nothing of this being nonsense."

"But it is!"

"Yes, yes. But God forbid they should hear you say something like that." Nathaniel Ingersoll discreetly nodded toward a clump of people huddled by the meetinghouse. The men's black steeple-crowned hats poked darkly at the winter sky.

"But evil hands, Nathaniel? Not here."

"Not another word, Virginia!"

Evil hands, Mary knew, meant one thing. It meant witchcraft.

There had never been any witchcraft around

Salem. In Boston there had been cases, and some in Marblehead years before, and Mary thought she remembered her parents talking about cases down in Connecticut. But here in Salem! It was unthinkable. Unimaginable. Yet at the same time, Mary felt a little surge of excitement. It was an excitement mixed with dread. How might they be, these invisible spirits that rode the air currents besieging innocents? Could she defend herself if one seized her? Would she really hurl herself into a fire?

Then Mary heard her mother's voice. There was a raw fear in it, something she had never heard before. "This is terrible! This is terrible!" her mother was saying as she looked across the road, observing two clutches of people who stood at different ends of the meetinghouse.

"This, I fear, is just the beginning, Virginia."

What did he mean, Mary wondered, as she watched the hunched shadow of John Indian slide across a remnant patch of snow by the path to the front door.

"Lovely, lovely, my dear! Of course I can grow lupine. One doesn't have to be pressing the sea."

Rebecca Nurse sat propped up in her bed against a small mountain of pillows. Francis and Rebecca Nurse's house was a beautiful, sturdily built old place. To the side was a flax garden, and out front an immense hedge of lilacs. Rebecca now looked wistfully out the window. "It's been a long winter, and here we are just beginning February, but you know I can almost see the buds on my lilac. Another month and they'll swell to the size of piglets' teeth."

Mary laughed at this. Goodwife Rebecca Nurse had the oddest and most vivid way of putting things. Frost was on the windowpane, but Mary tried to imagine little pink piglets sprouting from the hedge.

"So tell me the news of the village," Rebecca said.

Virginia bit her lip lightly in dismay.

"Oh, no!" Rebecca said, reading Virginia's pained expression. "Don't say it. Those girls again — more fits? The poor dears. Did they call Dr. Griggs? He's due here later today."

"I'm afraid, Rebecca."

"And what says he?"

Virginia clamped her eyes shut as she began to speak. "He says it is the evil hand upon them."

"Oh, stuff and nonsense." Rebecca Nurse flicked her hand in the air. "All these girls, save for little Betty Parris and Abigail Williams, are getting to that age. They're coming into their spring, like the maples out there." Rebecca gestured to a stand of trees through the leaded panes of the window facing north. "Their sap is rising. They want attention. We all want attention."

Mary nearly gulped out loud. She had never heard such frank talk.

"And they find the days long. They're not like you, young Mary. You're so busy helping your dear mother on the farm — you never have time to think about such things. Too busy for such nonsense, and that is the answer: They should be kept busier. When John Procter's girl servant Mary Warren was seized with fits, he sat her right down at the spinning wheel — had her spinning till kingdom come. That cured her fine. Very practical man, John Procter. It would be good if our Dr. Griggs would take a page from his book."

"But Goody Nurse," Virginia said, "from what I hear, the fits are so violent, the girls nearly hurt themselves."

"Nearly!" Rebecca raised her finger. "That is the difference: 'nearly,' but not quite. Has one of these children been burned when she has thrown herself into a fire? Has one broken a bone in twisting her limbs? But what attention they do get. My dear sister Sarah's husband was over at Ingersoll's Ordinary the other day when Abigail Williams fell down right on the floor in front of all the customers. Threw the place into an uproar. People running about trying to save her from choking, straightening out her limbs. She like't to bit a gentleman from Boston, I am told."

"No!" Virginia gasped.

"Yes." Rebecca Nurse nervously plucked at the coverlet on her bed. "And supposing the word does get to Boston. Remember the Witch Glover, four years ago?"

"What was that?" Mary asked.

"They hung a poor Irish washerwoman for causing fits in the children of a God-fearing mason. I believe his name was John Goodwin. But the fits didn't stop even after they hung the poor woman. So the Reverend Cotton Mather himself took the children into his own home to examine them, to perform what they called 'experiments' to root out the evil spirits. They said it worked. The Reverend Mather wrote a book about it. Imagine if our little Abigail could become an experiment for Dr. Mather? That would certainly make her feel like something grand."

"Oh, Goody Nurse! I must caution you. Deacon Ingersoll said we must mind our tongues."

"Yes, he is right. We must not talk this way, too freely, outside our homes."

As they left Rebecca Nurse's house, Mary's mind spun — spun with images of piglets blooming on lilac hedges, of stalks of lupine blowing in a field, of girls twisting and frothing and heaving themselves into fires as they wrestled with the invisible world of the Devil and his evil handmaidens, the witches. Was it not real in some way? How could it not be? Mary must see one of these fits for herself. She must hear the limbs cracking, see the heads spinning, the tongues lolling and slavering.

But they drove home in silence. She knew better than to trouble her mother with her curiosities and these dark thoughts.

CHAPTER
FIVE

That evening, a warm southwesterly breeze began to blow. The icicles that hung like glass spears from the eaves began to drip, and one could almost hear the snow melting in the barnyard. The earth made sucking, muddy sounds as it softened, released from winter's grip.

Mary and her mother had finished cleaning up the supper dishes, and the steady drip of icicles from the eaves seemed to beckon Mary outside. She picked up an apple from the barrel. "I'm going out to give Sass an apple. She was such a good old thing in the harness today. I'll give her a gift."

Virginia smiled. She knew her daughter longed for spring and summer, and even in February, with long months to go, she could not resist this teasing air that hinted at warmer days.

"Remember your cloak, Mary. It's not May yet." For indeed Mary had begun to leave with nothing more than a knit shawl over her shoulders.

"Oh, dear!" She feigned surprise. But her mother knew better. Mary most likely had intended to go out and deny any chill in the air, keeping herself warm with thoughts of summer.

Sass stood by the rail of the fence in the barnyard.

"Here, old gal," Mary clucked. "Over here, Sweet Sass. I brought you a lovely apple."

The big draft horse sighed, sputtered a thin mist through her huge, speckled nostrils, and ambled over to where Mary perched on the fence.

As the horse munched on the apple, Mary scanned the sky. She was learning the stars. She knew that sailors navigated by the configurations of the stars in the heavens. She was coming to know their patterns and knew that soon familiar figures would begin to rise against the blackness.

Caleb had told her the names of some. There was one she especially liked, Auriga, the Charioteer, and then there was the one called the Swan. But first, she always looked for the Big Bear and then the Little Bear, or as they were more often called, the Big and the Little Dipper. If she followed the handle of the Little Dipper straight out, she could find Polaris, the star that never moved. This was the star sailors looked for.

Caleb had told her that sailors figured a ship's position at sea by measuring stars' positions through numbers and arithmetic. It was unimaginable that numbers could be used for anything except counting up earthly things. To Mary, it was unutterably wonderful and mysterious that sailors could figure out where they were by a star. She supposed it might be considered a kind of magic, a little sorcery. But that was one she would definitely like to know how to work.

And then her mind stopped. It was as if a shade had been drawn. She remembered the knots of people on the corner in the village, dark and whispering. She remembered what Deacon Ingersoll had warned: they must mind their tongues that the girls' afflictions were all nonsense. Must she, Mary Chase, now mind her thoughts as well as her tongue? Was this what had happened to the poor afflicted girls? Had they not minded their thoughts, and perhaps in the looseness of their minds, the evil hand had seized their brains like a fever? Must she never dare to think about stars and the mystery of their numbers and their transit across the skies? Must she always think about numbers only for counting eggs and chickens and measuring fields and weighing grain? How did one tell oneself to stop thinking about something? It seemed nearly impossible. But if she couldn't stop, would the evil hand come upon her? Would the Tall Man, the demon with his big black book, come and make her sign?

Mary had heard talk of the Man and his book. They said he leaped upon you, and in the book all the verses of the Bible were turned inside out; words and letters were written upside down in ways that made terrible spells and bound you to the Devil himself. The Tall Man was the Devil's agent, and it was he whom the witches obeyed. She had heard stories, but they had, until now, just been stories.

No more.

CHAPTER

SIX

L ong before Gilly swung open the gate, Mary had been roused by her mother. The sow had given birth early to eight piglets. A sudden change of weather often brought on early births.

Virginia was watchful at these times. She had checked long before dawn, and sure enough, there in the stall, the eighth piglet was just slipping out as Virginia walked in. Two were born dead, and at least two were true runts. She knew the mother would kill the runts, and Virginia needed all the pigs she could raise. Salt pork was a main source of income. She sold it to Ingersoll's Ordinary as well as to the two taverns along the Ipswich Road — John Procter's, and another belonging to Joshua Rea. Bridget Bishop, who ran an unlicensed tavern where local youths drank cider and played shuffleboard, had also spoken to Virginia about buying pork. But Virginia was reluctant. Bridget's place was as rowdy as the bright red bodice she laced over her dark, homespun dress.

In any case, there was certainly a market for the

Chases' pork, and Virginia did not want to lose any. She scooped up the runts and tucked them into her dress. They weren't getting the warmth they needed, and if they survived the next half hour, they would also need milk. She and Mary would have to sop them. They'd never get a teat on that sow.

There was so much to be done. Mary had to go to Goody Dawson's to take the spun wool. The woman's arthritis was so bad, she could no longer spin herself, and Virginia did it for her in exchange for a special strain of seed potatoes that Goodman Dawson raised. Then there was the fence repair. Gilly had been so slow with it that Mary was going to have to help him. As well, Virginia had spinning to do for herself, and she had to get to the loom, for Caleb needed a new tunic. All of these chores — weaving, spinning, fence repair, milking, churning — would have to be done while carrying the piglets around, close to their own body heat, and then stopping to sop them several times each hour.

"Mary, dear," Virginia whispered softly. She leaned over her sleeping daughter. Mary smelled the unmistakable wet, warmish stink of piglets. She opened her eyes.

"Oh, Ma. The sow came on with the piglets."

"Yes, indeed. Two are dead, but I have two little runts here in my bodice."

Mary sat bolt upright. "None others alive?"

"Oh yes, dear, four out there are quite fine for coming so early."

"Why is it always the pigs that get upset by this weather?"

"Pigs are more sensitive than one would think, and they are smarter than most animals."

"If they were all that smart, they wouldn't get born in February." Mary was out of bed and pulling on her stockings.

The piglets survived the first half hour, and Mary came back in with a pan of milk. Her mother had the sopping rags ready. They sat by the fire and dipped the corners into the warm milk, then, with their fingers, worked open the piglets' tiny jaws and introduced the soaked cloth. One had to teach a piglet this young how to suck, rub its little throat to stimulate its muscles, blow soft streams of air on its face to keep it warm, to keep it alert. Within five minutes there were tiny pulls on the cloth. The trick was not to interrupt the sucking when one cloth was dry, but to have another ready to insert. And all the while, one had to rub their throats and their stomachs to make sure the milk got down.

All morning long, Mary and her mother went about their work with the piglet runts tucked in close to their skin. It would have to be this way for a few days if the pigs were to survive. Then, after three or four days, they would be able to put them in a box by the hearth.

By mid-morning of that day, every icicle had melted, and roads were turning to mud. Mary had been helping Gilly with some fencing, but he was moving at a very slow speed. For every fence post that Gilly shimmed, Mary shimmed two, and she was also having to break to sop the piglet. She looked down the fence line. Now what was he doing?

"Gilly, you having trouble?"

"No, Mary, just my boots." He was bent over, tying something on them.

"What are you doing?" she asked, walking up to him.

"Oh, I'm just taking good care of your father's boots." He was tying burlap around them with twine.

"But Gilly, it's thick with mud out here. These boots are mud boots, and Pa wore them in the mud. So you can, too."

"But then they might not work."

"What do you mean, work?"

Gilly lowered his eyes. He sucked in his mouth and seemed to chew on it. Why had he said that? They would think he was foolish. But he felt the change, he did — every time he put on Jacob

Chase's boots, the thoughts came quicker and more orderly, and he could maybe speak a little more smoothly. He could explain all that right now, very directly, but she might laugh. Oh, and he didn't want the Chase womenfolk to laugh at him. That would be terrible. Now, what was Mary saying?

"But they are work boots, Gilly. Pa worked in them. He didn't mind them getting dirty. That's what work boots are for."

"But I'd feel so terrible, Mary, if something happened to them."

"Nothing will happen to them except good, hard work and plain old mud. You can scrape off the mud at the end of the day, and I'll give you some oil to rub them down with, and a nice, soft piece of fleece."

"You will?" The crumpled face looked into hers. It was difficult for Mary to imagine how simple Gilly's mind was.

She felt the little runt squirm against her. Time to sop him again. There were so many things that needed taking care of. Maybe Rebecca Nurse was right. Maybe those girls had fits because there wasn't anything else to fill up their days. But they were servant girls, and servant girls were kept plenty busy. Not as busy as this, Mary thought as she sat on a rock. Her hem dipped in the mud while she sopped the pig. She looked at the next fence post to be shimmed. Could she fit the blades of wood in that hole? It looked fairly big.

She wished she could think of this fence as a ship, and instead of shimming she'd be scarfing, learning from a carpenter like Master Jeremy. But the fence was just a fence, and Gilly was no Jeremy. That was the plain and simple truth.

CHAPTER
SEVEN

"It is just as I thought. Yes. They didn't need Dr. Griggs to tell them it was the evil hand. And now the Reverend Hale's coming down from Beverly. But you know when there were those rumors about Bridget Bishop and her sorceries, the Reverend Hale went soft." Goodwife Dawson clicked her tongue disapprovingly. "But he does know the invisible world. He has many great books on it with pictures of them all."

"Who all?" Mary asked.

"The familiars, of course, my dear. And the fiends that go by land and air and sea, the incubi and the succubi, the wizards of the night, the witches of hearth and hell. Oh yes, he's got pictures of them all." Goody Dawson paused again and peered intently at Mary. Then she picked up a skein of wool and examined it. "My, my. Your mother does a fine piece of work with this wool." She held up the skein to the window's light and drew out several inches.

"Who else is coming?" Mary asked.

"Well, from Salem Town, the Reverend Nicholas

Noyes will be coming, but then you never know with those folks over in Salem Town. I think they should call for the Reverend Cotton Mather from Boston."

"But what are they to do, all these reverends?"

Goody Dawson dropped the skein and her hands into her lap and stared at Mary as if she were the simplest person on earth, simpler even than Gilly. "Well, what do you think? They must find out who is tormenting the poor things. These are the Devil's people; these witches signed in the black book."

"But how do the girls know?" Mary asked.

"Well, if the specter looks like someone, that's proof enough as to who the witch is. Only a person in league with the Devil has the power to send his spirit to twist innocents' limbs. I tell you, Mary dear, I could almost see the dreadful hands on poor little Ann Putnam myself when she was so twisted, and with Abigail Williams, too."

"But could you see the face?"

"No, no, of course not, dear, because I was not the afflicted one. But you can wager that Abigail and Ann could. They must be coaxed to tell. The witches will threaten them with death and worse, most likely, once their names are spoken."

Goody Dawson drew up her stout frame and thrust her chest out with great self-importance. "Then there can be proceedings once the names are named." Her puffy cheeks jiggled a bit as the word "proceedings" came out of the tiny, nearly invisible mouth. It was a word she obviously enjoyed saying. It seemed as if the very act of saying such a word made Goody Dawson feel superior, almost like a magistrate or a councillor. "It'll be a hard job getting the names out. There is a way, though." She dropped her voice and seemed to mumble into the skein of yarn.

"What way is that?" Mary asked.

"I was talking with Goody Sibley about it the other day. You bake a rye cake using the urine of the afflicted girls and feed it to a dog. The dog begins to act strangely toward the girls, and this brings out the names of the witches. They have to say them. The names scald their tongues until they spit them out — just like that." Goody Dawson clapped her two fat little hands in the air.

Suddenly Mary wanted to get out, get away from Goody Dawson and all her talk.

Ten minutes later she was well down the road. It was a blessed relief to hear only the suck of the mud on her boots. She saw the blue flash of two jays in an apple tree. "Soon it will be spring. Soon it will be spring!"

The words kept running through her head. But she knew it wasn't true. It was just an unseasonably warm day early in February. It was, in fact, the worst kind of day. It was a tease. The crocuses might be coaxed out very early just like the piglets, and then the weather could change; a killing blizzard might sweep the land, followed by an icy nor'easter, and everything would die.

She wondered how the runt was doing — the one she had left with her mother while she did this errand. Tomorrow, she promised herself, if the runt lived, she would tuck it in her bodice and take it to show Caleb. It had been nearly two weeks since she had last seen him, and her mother should have his new tunic finished.

She walked home, again trying not to think of things like urine cakes and black books with iron clasps, and gossipy old ladies. She wanted to think about the spring. But she was deeply suspicious of the sun, which shone so brightly now in the almost blue New England sky. And if she were to see a crocus or the shoot of an early daffodil, oh, how she would tell it to go back, go back! For this was not the time of birth, or renewal. This was still a dying time in a long winter yet to come.

CHAPTER
EIGHT

"I feel like Jonah. This is like sitting in the belly of a whale," Mary said to her brother Caleb.

"It was barely a month ago that we laid the keel; now look how far we've come."

"I want to see everything you've scarfed. You say it's not just the stem, it's the ribs, too?"

"Yes. You see right down there? That's the one I just finished this morning, and they put it in place."

Mary got up and followed her brother. She was careful not to trip, for the floors of the ship were yet to be laid, and the gaps between ribs were deep. Caleb ran his hand over one of the ribs. "You see, the first point of scarfing is right here, where the rib begins to curve up."

Mary traced the seam with her finger, where the two pieces of wood had been cut at mirror angles to be joined tightly. "It's so perfect, the cutting."

"The cutting is the easy part," Caleb said and drew his face closer to the wood. "It's shaping the two ends so they fit and overlap just right that is hard."

Caleb squinted as he examined his work. His clear gray eyes grew more intense, and then he walked over to the next rib and squinted again. "This is Master Jeremy's. It's a fine lot better."

Mary came over to look at the rib. "I can't tell the difference," she said.

"You're not apprenticed to a master."

Mary bit her lip and cast down her eyes.

"What's the matter, Mary? What's got you today? It's almost like spring these past two days. You should be happy."

"It's not like spring at all, Caleb." The words spurted out. She was surprised by her own vehemence.

Caleb recoiled slightly. His brow knitted. This was not like Mary.

"You don't know what spring is like, especially not this spring — if it ever comes. You are in here, always." She gestured with her hand to the soaring ribs of the brigantine. "You are always here with the smell of hard wood, and the sawdust, and the noise of the tools, and there is no weather, no season in here."

"What are you talking about?"

Mary looked at him. Although Caleb was almost three years older and a great deal taller, he suddenly seemed younger to her. His smokey-brown hair had wood curls in it, and his dark gray eyes were like the clearest pools in the woods. It didn't matter that he had the beginnings of a mustache. She only saw his freckles, and they stood out now against the pallor of his face. His skin had not seen the sunlight for nearly a year of working all day in the boat sheds of the Storey shipyard. Did he know anything of the troubles?

"Have you heard about what is happening in Salem Village?" Mary asked. "The girls and their afflictions?"

"Oh . . . oh, yes. I did hear something about one of the Parris girls — was it the niece?"

"Yes. Abigail, as well as little Betty, and now Ann Putnam and Mary Walcott, Susannah Sheldon, Elizabeth Hubbard, and Elizabeth Booth." Mary felt something swell like a dry sob at the back of her throat. Her heart was racing. "Oh, there's a passel of them taken with the fits. It's terrible." The words came out now in a rush. "And they called in Dr. Griggs, and he is saying it's the evil hand, and now they're calling in the Reverend Hale from Beverly and the Reverend Noyes from here in Salem Town — they being such experts, you know."

"Experts on what?"

"Witchcraft, Caleb. Witchcraft — they think witches and all sorts of fiends are flying around, tormenting the girls. And they're going to get the girls to name them, and Goody Dawson has a certain way — you take the urine of the girls and bake it into a rye cake and then feed it to a dog."

"What are you talking about?" Caleb was stunned. He had never seen his sister this way. Her mouth was going like a runaway horse.

"Witchcraft."

"But it's crazy. How can they go about naming things they can't see?"

"I don't know. I don't know, Caleb. But you have heard of it happening in other places, haven't you?"

"Why yes, yes, down Boston way and Connecticut, and maybe there was something going on over in Marblehead, but still, not here. . . ."

"Yes, here!"

"But you don't think so, nor does Mother."

"I don't know what I think anymore. They say the girls' fits are terrible, something to behold that you cannot imagine, limbs being twisted this way and that. But John Procter and Rebecca Nurse think the girls just need to be whipped or set to work."

"Well, I wouldn't get so worried about it, Mary. You look a fright when you get going that way. I've never seen you like this before."

"It's fine for you to say, Caleb. You are far from it."

She stopped and looked around. The ribs of larchwood swept in graceful curves toward the ceiling. Sweet-smelling wood dust permeated the air.

The careful marks on the white pine of the first floorboard to be laid were fine and crisp. This was a place of order, of harmony, of careful measurement and craft. There were no mysteries from an invisible world of succubi and wizards. You use a hand ax wrong, you lose a finger; you use it right, and you make a piece that is a good fit and helps a ship sail in any sea. Such was the moral order of the shipyard. There were no demons to blame. There were only good tools to be handled well and skills to be honed. This was a simple place, a good place, and suddenly it struck Mary with unexpected force that if heaven could be like this place, it would be good enough for her. She should not have brought her talk of witchcraft and urine cakes, of hysterical girls and fiends, into such a place as this.

"I am sorry, Caleb."

"What are you sorry for?"

"For bringing you the troubles from Salem Village — a silly place. I am sorry."

Caleb's eyes grew cloudy. He did not like to hear his sister apologizing in this way. It wasn't like Mary to have such an outburst, and if she did, there must be good reason. He hoped the farm wasn't becoming too difficult for her and his mother. If they could only hang on another two years, he would be able to come back and help them a bit more, and he would be making money by then. They could hire more help.

No, he didn't like it at all, and this talk of witch-craft was unsettling. Mary had said the Reverend Noyes was going over to Salem Village. Caleb had gone to meeting just a few times. He had no real impression of the man. Where Caleb lived, in Salem Town, people did not go to meeting every single Wednesday and Sunday as faithfully as they did in the village, and they did not keep track of attendance. But perhaps he should go with his mother and Mary to a Wednesday or Sunday service in the village. Perhaps he could learn more about the strange affliction. He certainly didn't want his sister to catch it.

CHAPTER
NINE

The ministers sat like dark crows at the front of the meetinghouse. Mary recognized the one she had encountered two days before when she had been coming home from visiting Caleb. She had passed him on the Ipswich Road. He had been carefully guiding his nag through the slush and mud.

So this was the Reverend Hale, Mary thought, the very one with the books that Goody Dawson had spoken of, the books with the portraits of the Devil's familiars. According to folks in the village, he was a scientist of sorts. For he knew as much about the wizards and witches as Dr. Griggs knew about the human body. He possessed a great and terrible knowledge. And he knew the symptoms, and the signs and "procedures" for dealing with the fiends.

When Mary had met him on the road, he had stopped his nag to ask directions to Ingersoll's Ordinary. He had then smiled at her in a condescending way, and asked if she were of the village.

"No, sir. I live just a piece up the road."

"Where do you worship?"

"At the meetinghouse in the village."

"And you go with great regularity?"

"As much as possible, sir, as my mother is widowed, and my brother is apprenticed, and she and I must work the farm ourselves — but never on Sabbath. Sometimes, however, it is difficult to get into meeting, but then we do pray in the house."

"But your house is not holy. It is not a church, and there is not an ordained minister."

Mary did not know how to answer him. He was not that old, but his skin was drawn tight, and his eyes burned brightly. Eagerly he leaned over the side of his carriage while the nag pawed the mud. "You are not one of the afflicted children, are you?"

"Oh, no, sir — never!"

A harsh look slashed the tight skin of his face. "How can you be sure?" he asked. "Do you have a special knowledge, a special dispensation from this affliction?"

"Oh, no, sir — no. I know nothing."

He smiled slightly. "As it should be. And tell me, child, have you been baptized?"

"Oh, most certainly."

And there the interview on the muddy road had ended. But she remembered every dreadful word of it, and never had she been so frightened by an adult. Now this same man sat in the front of the room. Mary shrank between her mother and Caleb. She was so pleased that Caleb had come to meeting, this meeting in particular.

The day after the ministers from the outlying towns and villages had arrived, they had declared that the next day would be a day of prayer and fasting. In the interim, they had carefully interrogated each of the afflicted girls and would continue to do so after this day of prayer.

So far, no witches had been named. But she had heard a rumor that Tituba and her husband, John Indian, had indeed made the peculiar cake. She had heard this from Mary Warren, the girl who worked for John Procter and who had been one of the afflicted — until he set her to spinning and gave her a good whipping.

After the psalm was spoken, the Reverend Hale stood up and named his text from the Book of Isaiah:

"Shall the clay say to him that fashioneth it, what makest thou?

"Behold I have refined thee but not with silver; I have chosen thee in the furnace of affliction."

Suddenly there was a terrible screech, and Abigail Williams, the Reverend Parris's eleven-year-old niece, flung herself onto the floor. Her arms jerked, and her eyes rolled. She bashed her head against the pew. The eyes of the entire congregation were riveted on the writhing child.

The Reverend Hale fell silent and stared in disbelief along with the rest of the congregation. The Reverend and Mrs. Parris rushed to their niece's side. The reverend held down her flailing legs while his wife grabbed frantically at her arms.

"Hush! Hush, child!" they implored as they wrestled with limbs that appeared to take on lives of their own.

Finally, after several minutes, the Parrises managed to straighten their niece's arms and legs. Abigail became tranquil and then totally limp. The Reverend Parris lifted her onto the pew, where she leaned listlessly against her aunt. But everyone watched her warily as the Reverend Hale resumed his text.

No sooner had he spoken the Lord's name than young Ann Putnam began a strange gurgling. She stood up, right behind Mary and Caleb. The sound came as a dreadful watery burble, as if a ship had sprung a leak. Mary and Caleb wheeled about.

Ann was now howling and pointing toward the rafters of the meetinghouse. Her entire body was stiff as a board. Then Abigail once more began twitching and set up a terrible shrieking, as if being touched by a hot iron. There was a whoop from Ann, who until that moment had been rigid. Now she began to jerk her limbs in an antic dance while hitting herself.

"Look!" cried Ann Putnam senior. "The fiend pinches her with its hot claws!"

And Mary did indeed believe she could see long, angry marks scraping across young Ann's neck.

The outbursts continued through the rest of the service. The congregation's eyes were rarely on the minister. When the service finally concluded, all the ministers swept out of the room and headed for the Parris house.

"They'll get them now," Goody Dawson was saying in a hot whisper on the meetinghouse steps.

"I cannot believe it!" said Goody Cloyce.

"Believe what?" Goody Dawson asked sharply. "You saw it! You saw it with your own eyes."

"Yes, yes," Goody Cloyce said quietly. "I saw a travesty made of a divine service. Come, let us go," she said to her older sister, Rebecca Nurse. And the two women sailed out like sprightly ships in a smart breeze.

Mary stared after them.

"What do you think of that, Virginia?" Goody Dawson turned to ask.

"I think they are wise and Godly souls," Virginia said, looking after the two women. "And I think we best be on our way, children."

"Mark my words: We shall know their names, and by tomorrow, witches will be cried out," Goodwife Dawson called. The words floated off from her invisible mouth and hung in the chilly morning air.

CHAPTER
TEN

C aleb Chase lingered behind. Since he had to go back to Salem Town that evening, he would not be accompanying his mother and sister home to the farm. Caleb knew that at the corner of the Parris's house was a lilac bush, dense even when leafless in winter, and between the lilac bush and the house was a small depression, a cellar well that was dug down to the foundation. He wanted to see more.

Once upon a time, he had thought Abigail Williams was the prettiest, gentlest girl he'd ever met. He simply could not believe what he had seen in the meetinghouse. Even before today's fits began, she had seemed changed. When they had seen each other on the steps, she had not so much as bid him hello after all his months away.

Now Caleb pressed close to the house and looked through the leaded panes. The Putnams and their daughter, Ann, were inside, along with Mercy Lewis and Mary Walcott. Mary Warren was not there, for John Procter would have none of this nonsense. He had taken her back home to read the

Bible on the Sabbath, spin the next Monday, and be beaten on Tuesday if any fits set in.

Mrs. Parris sat erect and stunned as she held poor, limp Betty in her arms. The ministers were hovering over the two. Caleb could see the Reverend Parris kneeling in prayer in front of his daughter.

"Can you hear me, Betty, dear?" the Reverend Parris was saying very loudly. "Tell us, dear, who afflicts you." Then he turned away abruptly. His face was a mask of fear. He tore at his hair. "My child! My child is dying!"

The Reverend Noyes approached. "Tell us, child. Tell us."

Then something happened or was said that Caleb could not make out. He saw the Reverend Parris turn back suddenly toward his wife and Betty; the circle of people tightened around the child.

A terrible moan rose up: "Tituba! Tituba!" The word sailed out from the dark, shingled house. To Caleb it would forever be mysterious whether that name cried out was an accusation or a call for help.

But just then, as the last syllable of the name curled through the air, he saw young Ann Putnam stand up straight and stare directly at him through the leaded panes. Her face was twitching, and one eye ticked madly. Caleb's heart seized. She pointed right at him.

"It is Tituba! It is Tituba!" she screamed. Caleb

jumped into the cellar well and crouched. But he heard no sound of footsteps above. Just more screams. He dared to raise up a bit, his eye barely an inch above the sill.

Now Abigail had thrown herself onto the floor, calling "Tituba!" until the air itself was convulsed with the rhythm of the slave's name cried out again and again by hysterical girls.

Then Tituba appeared in the doorway. Her bronze face glowed under her colorful turban. She was wringing her hands. "My babies, my babies!" she moaned.

Both Abigail and Betty ran to cower in a corner. It was Ann Putnam who shrieked a new name in a very high-pitched but clear voice: "Sarah Good!" And then the girls began to run wildly through the room, chanting, "Goody Good! Goody Good! Goody Good!"

By the time Caleb crawled out from under the lilac, a third name had been cried out. It was that of Sarah Osburne.

By the following day, the last day of February, warrants for all three women had been issued. Tituba, Sarah Good, and Sarah Osburne had been arrested by the constables, who were ordered to bring them to Nathaniel Ingersoll's Ordinary the next day: March 1, 1692.

* * *

That evening, as Caleb Chase lay on his cot in the back of one of the toolsheds of the shipyard, he did not think about the names of the accused witches, or how terrible the shrieking had been. Nor did he reflect on the strange contortions of the girls' bodies. Rather he thought about their faces — Abigail's, little Betty's, Ann Putnam's, Mary Walcott's, and Mercy Lewis's. Their faces were stranger than any twisted limbs, any frothing of the mouth, or shrill, piercing cries.

Their faces had become something that was not quite human.

CHAPTER
ELEVEN

She was a powerful old hag, dark and leathery, with one rheumy eye that seemed never to focus but still saw everything. She clenched the pipe between her few teeth. Her matted hair was filthy with the grime of sleeping outdoors or in the stalls of animals.

Sarah Good had known for years that people disliked her, even reviled her. People would cross the street to avoid Sarah and her stench as much as to get away from her begging. But now they were all in the same room with her. The beast had been caged. And as she looked out at them, despite her confused and muddled state of mind, something became very clear to her: These people feared her.

The day before, one day after the girls had cried out the names of their tormentors, Tituba, Sarah Good, and Sarah Osburne had been arrested, although each one had declared her innocence. Originally, the examinations of the accused witches were supposed to be held at Nathaniel Ingersoll's Ordinary, but the crowds were too large. Now the afflicted girls sat in the front-row seats across from the magistrates' table in the meetinghouse. Mary Chase and her mother were seated near the rear of the room.

What indeed was this magistrate talking about, Sarah Good wondered. For the fifth time he had asked this question: "Why do you torment these children?"

"I scorn it," she said. She spoke out angrily, not muttering.

"Who do you employ to torment the children?"

"I employ nobody."

"How came they thus tormented?"

"I do not know." She jammed the pipe farther into her mouth.

"And it has been said that when you go away from a house after begging, you mutter, and cows have died from your mutterings."

At this point, Mary saw Goody Dawson turn to her husband and nod her head with a smug look of approval. Mary remembered that Goody Dawson did have a cow die last spring. Had Sarah come a-begging then? But she had come to the Chases' house, and nothing like that had ever happened.

"What is it that you say when you go away muttering from a person's house?"

"I will say my commandments."

"What commandment is it? Who do you serve?"

"It is God," Sarah Good said.

"But you torment the children." Magistrate

Hathorne did not ask this as a question. He stated it as a fact. "Look at them now, Goody Good. They told us that you hurt them only this morning."

A terrible bark rent the air and seemed to go right up Mary's spine. Indeed she thought that perhaps Sarah's spirit had lashed out like a whip, stinging her. But then she realized that it was Abigail Williams. Abigail had fallen down upon the floor. Snapping and growling, the girl began biting at the legs of the table where the magistrates sat.

Ann Putnam now began to make gagging noises, and several of the other girls fell to the floor writhing, except for Betty Parris, who was frozen in her seat with her eyes locked in a terrible stare. The girls had suddenly been gripped in a most horrible torture that streamed from the evil spirit of Sarah Good — whose leathery face showed not a whit of sympathy for them.

"She has bitten them! See Mary Warren's hand," someone cried out.

Virginia and Mary craned their necks to look toward the front of the room. Mary Warren lifted her hand; indeed there was blood on it.

Sarah Good seemed unimpressed with her powers. She continued to mutter and scowl.

"It was Sarah that brought the smallpox," a voice cried out. "Two winters ago. It was Sarah!"

"Yes, and my dog went mad the night I gave Sarah some bread when she came a-begging!"

shouted another voice over the howls and shrieks of the girls.

Finally, when the fits had subsided and when Magistrate Hathorne had asked for the seventh or eighth time who it was then who tormented the girls, Sarah Good hissed, "It was Sarah Osburne."

Now Sarah Osburne was led before the assembly. Goody Osburne looked frail and quite broken. Hathorne began the questioning.

"What evil spirit have you familiarity with?"

"None." She spoke quietly. There was no anger as there had been with Sarah Good — only quiet dismay.

"Have you made no contract with the Devil?"

"No. I never saw the Devil in my life."

"Why do you hurt these children?"

The question seemed unfair to Mary Chase, even if Sarah Good had finally said that Sarah Osburne had hurt the girls. It was as if Sarah Osburne had already been judged guilty, and Hathorne was taking the word of a poor muddled beggar now for the truth.

But Sarah Osburne, for all her frailness, stood up to the magistrate. Firmly and repeatedly she denied it all, ever knowing the Devil, ever hurting the children. She knew none of the Devil's agents, his familiars as they called them.

But then Magistrate Hathorne presented a tricky

question. "It has been said by some that you have said you would never believe that lying spirit anymore. What lying spirit is this? Has the Devil ever deceived you, and been false to you?" Mary felt her mother tense beside her. What was Hathorne doing? Had not the woman just said that she never had seen the Devil in her life?

"I never did see the Devil." She spoke wearily while looking straight ahead.

"What lying spirit was it, then?"

"It was a voice I thought I heard."

Mary's heart sank. She knew this would be the beginning of the end for Sarah Osburne. And Hathorne knew it, too. He turned his back dramatically on the woman and faced the people. He raised one dark eyebrow.

"What did it say to you?" he thundered.

"That I should go no more to meeting; but I said I would, and did go the next Sabbath-day."

"Were you never tempted further?" The eyebrow rose still higher. Hathorne turned his face toward a window so his profile was presented to the people. The sunlight streaming through limned his sharply cut features. His black robes draped down like the wings of an immense crow. Mary could not take her eyes off him, nor could the rest of the people.

"Why did you yield thus far to the Devil as to never go to meeting since, for indeed you have been absent of late?"

Something in Mary wanted to stop him; wanted to say no, this is not fair. He was trapping Sarah Osburne. "But Mother," Mary whispered, leaning toward her mother's ear, "Goody Osburne has been sick for all these last two winters; that is why she missed."

It did not matter that Goody Osburne had been sick, or that Sarah Good had only muttered the commandments and sometimes a psalm. A mere look from one of these women sent the afflicted girls into horrible contortions.

It was now Tituba's turn. She swept into the room, a dark majestic presence in her saffron-and-white turban. Her high cheekbones gleamed, and her dark eyes focused above the heads of the afflicted girls.

Tituba wasted no time. Within seconds after her testimony began, a hush fell upon the court and lasted for twenty minutes as she spun a tale that every villager was eager to hear; for at last this was the truth. And how colorful this truth was, what a tincture of scarlet it added to their drab, homespun lives of work and toil, prayer and plainness.

"Sometimes it is like a hog, and sometimes it is like a great dog," spoke Tituba. Mary gasped and felt her mother's hand tighten on her own. Tituba's eyes slid around the room, taking in the effect her responses had on the people who were watching.

"What did it say to you?" Hathorne asked.

"The black dog said, 'Serve me, serve me,' but I said, 'I am afraid.' He said if I didn't serve, he would do worse to me."

"What else have you seen?"

"Two cats: a red cat and a black cat."

The room grew even more hushed as the people leaned forward to hear better.

"What did they say to you?"

" 'Serve me,' " she said. " 'To hurt the children.' "

"Did you not pinch Elizabeth Hubbard this morning?"

"The man brought her to me and made me pinch her."

There was now a loud gasp, then a deep murmur that rolled through the audience like distant thunder. Magistrate Hathorne lifted his dark eyes and slowly, very slowly, looked across the room into the faces of the people. To Mary he seemed to be saying, "See! See! The Devil is here in Salem Village. His familiars — the dogs, the cats — work for this woman, pinching and harassing your children."

But Mary could not understand it. Tituba herself, like the others, had denied it. When the magistrate first had asked, "What evil spirit have you familiarity with?" she had answered, "None." "Why do you hurt them?" "I do not hurt them. The Devil for aught I know." For the first few minutes she had denied as the others had, but then her testimony had turned. In one split second she began

70

to weave an incredible tale describing precisely how the Devil came to her.

This was not at all like Goody Good, who blamed Sarah Osburne after being worn down by the magistrate. This was different. Tituba told her tale with enthusiasm, punctuating her story with gestures so fluid her hands seemed to move like dark fish through water. She cried out herself on Goody Good and Goody Osburne. Why? Why? wondered Mary. Was it because she was a slave, and she did not value her own life? Or did she value her life beyond what anyone could imagine for a slave? Did she indeed see something the others did not?

Tituba told of seeing a yellow bird that she claimed was the familiar of Sarah Osburne. Moreover, she had seen the Tall Man from Boston, and they — the man, the cats, and the witches — had flown over the countryside for their meetings in lonely fields and deep woods. Yes, yes. The afflicted girls all agreed they had seen them flying; and Elizabeth Hubbard had been tormented by the wolf that Tituba described, and Ann Putnam knew the terrible little yellow bird. And, worst of all, Tituba said that there were two more witches still at large, but alas — she did not know them.

"Yes, there are two more!" cried Abigail and Ann Putnam. "They come and pinch at the dawn!"

The constables hauled all three of the women off to Ipswich Prison, north of Salem Village. The people were relieved that three of the witches were now locked in irons, but it seemed even more dreadful that two unseen, unnamed ones were still at large. Who were they? Who were their familiars? Did they have cats, or roosters? Or was there another wolf lurking in the forests?

CHAPTER
TWELVE

Mary and her mother rode home in silence. Not one word was spoken. Her mother seemed only too anxious to get out of the village and had not lingered on the meetinghouse steps to speak with Goody Dawson, who was more than eager to tell about how her cow had died last spring after Sarah Good's visit.

Mary, however, was thinking about a sharp exchange she had overheard just as they were leaving. It had been between Francis Nurse, Rebecca's husband, and Thomas Putnam. Putnam had apparently been cutting firewood for the parsonage.

"It's bad enough," fumed Francis, "that you deed the parsonage to the Reverend Parris for life and that of his heirs, but you shall not cut wood from my land to give to him as well."

"It's not your land, has never been your land, Francis. That is Putnam land, no matter what the Topsfield authorities say. That land lies within the parish of Salem Village."

What were they talking about? Mary wondered.

And old Francis Nurse was such a gentle soul. It shocked her to hear him speaking so fiercely.

"Mother," Mary said as their own house came into sight. "I heard Goodman Nurse and Goodman Putnam arguing about some firewood and where it had been cut."

"Oh, that!" said Virginia wearily. "That should be the least of our troubles. Yes, that land of Francis's has been disputed for these long years by the Putnams. They swear it is theirs, and since our village now has its own church and has become a proper parish, it seems that Thomas Putnam is laying stronger claim to it — all for the sake of the Reverend Parris and his family — the firewood, you know, is part of the reverend's salary contract."

"But what was it that Goodman Nurse said about deeding the house forever to the Reverend Parris?"

"Yes. Some people think he should have the house forever."

"But then what would happen if he were no longer our minister, and we had to get a new one? Where would the new one live?"

"Well, that's just the problem," Virginia said, looking out over the back of the horse she was driving. "It doesn't seem very practical, does it? I mean, we are not a rich village. We are not like Salem Town. We certainly cannot support two parsonage houses. I think it would have been better, perhaps, if we had never built our own meeting-house."

"But it's so much easier having our own nearby. It was so long to go to Salem Town, especially for those folks who do not live on the Ipswich Road like ourselves."

"Well, yes, the distance is shorter. However . . ." Virginia did not finish the thought.

"Oh, look at this little piglet!" Virginia said as they came into the barn to check the animals. "No, no, you fat little thing. You are no more a runt, and you cannot be carried around any longer, I tell you."

The two runts had survived, and the one Virginia had carried about had become extremely attached to her. However, it had grown rambunctious, and its little feet had scratched her one day, drawing blood and leaving a long, angry mark. Virginia had firmly reintroduced the pig to its mother. It had found a place among the teats, but it still clamored for Virginia.

At that moment, Gilly came in.

"Ah, Gilly, I did not expect you today," Virginia said. "I saw you at the meetinghouse and did not think you'd be here."

"Oh, yes, ma'am. It was quite a doing, wasn't it?"

His one eye shone fiercely and sparkled like a little moon in his dark face.

"If you came out here to discuss it, Gilly, I'll have none of it."

Gilly shrank back a bit, but only for a moment. Then he stood up a little straighter and squared his shoulders. "But, ma'am, I did indeed come to discuss it."

Virginia paused and opened her mouth slightly as if to speak. Was this insolence? Had she perhaps spoken too sharply? She must be careful to explain herself more clearly. Jacob had always said that one could never underestimate Gilly's simplicity. Jacob had been so wonderfully patient with Gilly. Oh, how she missed him now. Over time, the sharpness of her loss had subsided into a dull ache, but now she felt a sudden stab of it.

"Gilly," she said in a steady, patient voice, "today in the meetinghouse — what happened was very confusing and sad, I know."

"Confusing? Sad?" Gilly seemed indeed confused by these two words.

"Yes. Those poor women."

"Poor women?"

"Yes, Gilly. Those poor women. Poor Sarah Good, her mind a muddle; poor Sarah Osburne, so frail and sick."

"But she lived with that servant of hers before they was ever married," Gilly said quickly.

"That doesn't make her a witch, Gilly."

"But Magistrate Hathorne . . ."

"Magistrate Hathorne set out believing her guilty, making them all guilty by asking them unfair questions. One would only ask those questions if there had already been evidence of guilt."

"But they confessed, ma'am."

"They were forced to confess; they were led to confess. Such confessions are worth nothing. I daresay Martha Cory had the right idea. She did not even come, and she tried to prevent her husband from coming by taking away the saddle so he could not ride in. But I guess old Giles came anyway."

"And the Devil was there, ma'am, in that meetinghouse. You could see it with the poor afflicted girls."

"Oh yes, Gilly, the Devil was there all right, but he was not in the afflicted girls."

"Where was he, ma'am?"

"He was in the magistrates themselves!"

Now Gilly looked truly confused. "I don't understand you, not at all. And there are two other witches still about." He drew himself up tall again. "And I am here to protect you and Mary from them. Yes, ma'am, I promised your good husband that!"

It was no use to tell Gilly that there were no witches about. It was as if the simple fellow had to believe; and in believing it, he could also make himself feel even more important to Virginia and

Mary. Sometimes Virginia thought Jacob's death had been almost as difficult for Gilly as it had been for her and Caleb and Mary.

Jacob was practically the only employer Gilly had ever had, at least since he had walked all the way down from Maine many years before and convinced old man Storey to keep him about. When Jacob had still been a shipwright in the Storey Yard, he had taken pity on Gilly, who was given only the simplest tasks. But Jacob himself had taught Gilly how to care for the tools that he used as the master carpenter in the yard — how to sharpen the adzes, planes, and spokeshaves; to oil the augers and keep the caulking irons clean and free of rust. And then, when Jacob married Virginia, just a few years later, they bought their first bit of land to farm, and he brought Gilly out to the piece on the Ipswich Road to help clear it. Virginia remembered all of this.

But if Gilly had to believe in witches because he was so simple, what about the others? Virginia recalled the gleam in the villagers' faces. It was not just relief they were feeling. No, it was more a smug satisfaction. And just barely beneath the surface, she detected a kind of hunger — lust — yes, lust for more. There had been an almost holiday atmosphere in the village that morning. People had stopped to talk. They lingered at the roadway. They wore their best clothes. Work was far from their minds. The grayness of their lives had suddenly evaporated, and instead there had been color.

"You want to protect us?" Virginia asked in dismay.

"Yes, ma'am. It is my duty."

"But Gilly, how can you protect us?"

He paused a moment. He thought about the yellow bird Tituba had described and the hairy thing on two legs and the other with two heads. He wasn't sure how he might protect the Chase women against that; but there were the familiars — the red cat and the black cat, and then those unseen ones; and if the witch was a woman like Goody Osburne or Sarah Good, he might be able to wrestle with the spirit. It had been said that if you poured hot tallow down the throat of a demon woman, it stopped her quick enough. Yes, he could do that . . . if he stayed on the farm, he told Virginia. Not, of course, the way Goody Osburne let her servant stay in the house with her, but out back in the calving shed between the barn and the mud room.

Virginia saw no harm in it. There was no sense trying to convince Gilly that there were no witches; but if he could be made to feel constructive through protecting them, it was better than having him join the destruction she had seen growing in the village. Besides, it would be planting time soon, and better to have him nearby with all the work to be done.

CHAPTER
THIRTEEN

So Gilly stayed, sleeping in the calving shed. He slept on a straw pallet. He kept Jacob's boots near his head, and all night long the smell of leather crept into his nostrils. On warmer nights he fancied that he could even smell the faint, close odor of the sweat from his old master's feet. He had a notion that if he inhaled those perfumes long enough, a strange kind of alchemy would begin to work on his brain, and he would be changed from a simple man into one with complicated thoughts and ideas about planting crops and drawing diagrams for buildings. He might even learn how to see the wonderful shapes in wood that Jacob Chase had seen when the wood was still a living tree.

As a master shipwright, Jacob Chase had been able to look at a hackmatack or a poplar or a hickory and size up the "knees," or natural bends and points where the limbs angled into the trunks. He knew precisely how many knees he could get from a single tree. It might take him less than two or three minutes to figure it all out. And with this geometry, he could even imagine axles for wagons or lintels for houses.

Jacob Chase had been one who could see through his mind's eyes the secrets of the living world, master them, and from them build beautiful things. So each night when Gilly closed his eyes, he breathed in deeply the sweet fragrance of the boots, and he, Gilly Beales, imagined his mind growing stronger and one day filling up with big ideas and notions that would make him a rich man, a master of a small parcel of earth in a new land.

It was supposed to be Jacob whom he loved, and for Jacob he was here to protect Virginia and young Mary. But some time after that first day in March when he came with his few belongings to move into the calving shed, Gilly's feelings changed.

There had been an unseasonably warm day toward the middle of Gilly's second week. Southwesterly breezes had begun to blow, bringing with them warm, dry air. Virginia had told Mary to hang the wash out to dry on a line she had strung between two posts near the calving shed. It was the first time in many months that they had been able to hang the wash outside with the promise that it would be dry by evening.

Mary loved to watch the freshly laundered clothes billow in the gusts. Despite the fact that the colors were mostly dark, and the shapes were those of drawers and petticoats, bodices and sleeve pairs, chemises and underskirts, Mary could imagine top-sails and royals and spankers — all the canvas used to catch the wind and coax the great ships across the seas.

The clothes on that day did dry quickly in the warm breezes. Just after supper, in the early purple shadows of the evening, Mary went out to gather in the laundry. If she had been concentrating harder and the light were better, she might have noticed that an old pair of drawers was missing. But she did not.

Gilly had found those drawers, blown up against the door to his shed. Squinting with his one good eye, at first he did not know what the white thing was. Was it a hank of wool from the fleece of the sheep? But the sheep had not yet been shorn, and one never got a hank this big or this limp, for that matter. Fleece pieces blew like puffs of smoke in the wind.

He bent over to pick up the white thing, and he took it into the calving shed to examine. It was a strange-looking piece of work. It had been so long since Gilly had lived with a family or been around womenfolk that it took him several minutes to understand what he was looking at.

But then it slowly dawned on him. These were drawers, drawers that womenfolk tucked their legs in and pulled over their bottoms and up under their skirts. He giggled softly to himself. Then he looked at them again, intrigued. He would take them back in a minute, but they felt quite soft. He put them to his grizzled cheek. There was a wonderful fresh smell.

He knew that smell. It was the good soap Virginia Chase made. She threw in handfuls of clover and lavender and mixed it with the rendered fat and ashes. So the soap never smelled harsh like most. He would take it back tomorrow, but how nice to keep this soft thing near him through the night.

So that evening when he went to bed, he used the drawers for a pillow, and the sweet scent of the freshly laundered muslin swirled through the air. It seeped throughout the small shed, eclipsing the pungent leather smell of Jacob's boots. It was the sweetest fragrance Gilly had ever smelled. It stirred him in strange ways and made him forget his dreams of complicated thoughts and ideas for building things.

Gilly kept promising himself that he would return the drawers; he just needed them for one more night, and then he would give them back — or rather, he would just put them somewhere, perhaps on a bush as if they had blown there. But with each passing day, it became harder, and soon he had no intention of ever giving the drawers back, but indeed he longed for another day of fresh southwesterly breezes when Mary would again hang the laundry to dry, and perhaps another garment would fly away to Gilly's door.

This was a sign, Gilly decided, that it had been right that he had come here to live. Jacob Chase had been a fool to let himself catch his death of cold and leave Virginia by herself. But this was where he always got confused. It was Jacob he loved, wasn't it? Why was he finding himself getting angry with the man now?

Gilly did not understand his own feelings. And when he tried to understand them, he became so frustrated that he could not think at all. So he kept the drawers. And he would sometimes begin to imagine Virginia pulling them on. But it was a hard image to keep in his mind, for he couldn't recall ever seeing the bare or stockinged legs of a woman.

It was this realization that led Gilly Beales to think up his most complicated idea ever. The roof of the calving shed butted right up to the base of the dormer of Virginia Chase's bedroom.

CHAPTER
FOURTEEN

"Oh, I shan't go at all," Virginia said and snapped a piece of linen she had just taken off her loom. She began to smooth it on the table where she would finish off the edges with her needle.

"But there are still two witches tormenting the poor girls, ma'am. They are flying about as we speak."

"Well, I do not believe fasting and prayer are going to help. Three have already been wrongly accused. I am not going to pray and fast so more of this nonsense can be done, more falsehoods spread. But if you want to go, Gilly, I have no mind to keep you. You've worked hard."

"Thank you, ma'am, thank you." He wanted to say that it was only because of her that these witches should be caught; so that he could protect her — her lovely skin. But he could not think about that skin and those tapering legs that glowed, because when he did he got a raspy feeling in his chest, and his thoughts came too fast.

No sooner had Gilly left for the village than Mary

heard the creak of wagon wheels drawing up to their house. She hoped — she prayed — it was not Goody Dawson come to ask them, no doubt, if they were going to the day of prayer and fasting. With relief she heard the deep voices of two men.

Mary rushed to the window. "Mother," she called with delight. "It's Israel Porter and Daniel Andrews!"

"Oh!" Virginia said and laughed. "What pleasure!" She hurried to the door and opened it.

"Ah, you two good women are not in the town praying and fasting to catch those two demons!" said Daniel Andrews, a jovial, ruddy-faced man. He and his brother-in-law Israel Porter strode toward the hearth.

"Never heard such nonsense!" Virginia said emphatically.

"Well, here's some happy news. We'll be catching ourselves a landing wharf."

"Oh, Daniel, you did it! You bought the Frost Fish Brook landing." Virginia clapped her hands. "Ah, I'm so pleased for you."

"Be pleased for yourself, Goodwife Chase. Now you can take your salt pork, your potatoes and your flour, even your chickens to the village, put them on one of my shallops, and float them down to Salem Town where you can be sure there is a market."

"Oh! This was Jacob's dream!" Virginia sighed. "I am indeed so happy. Come sit down. Mary, fetch some cider. We must celebrate."

Mary poured the cider, and they raised their pewter mugs to wish Daniel Andrews well on his new venture. Then Israel Porter turned more serious. "I hear the Reverend Lawson is being called back to the fold."

"What? The Reverend Lawson is returning to Salem Village?" Virginia asked. "But the Reverend Parris is our minister now."

"With all this witch business, Deodat Lawson, no doubt with the Putnam family's consent, has been called in as a disinterested observer."

"Disinterested?" Virginia Chase's eyes widened in disbelief.

"Yes. My sentiments exactly. I daresay our former minister knows which side his bread is buttered on. And the Putnams have long been doing the buttering."

"And little Ann Putnam was among those who cried out against the three. Indeed, she was the one who cried out Sarah Osburne's name. Oh, this is not good, Israel. Mary, go fetch another jug of cider and check on that ewe in the yard."

Mary dutifully got up. She knew precisely what her mother was doing — getting her out of hearing range. This was often the way it was when a Porter came over. For as long as Mary could remember, there had been bad blood between the Porters and the Putnams. Her mother was very close to the Porters. The only Putnam she was truly friendly with was Joseph, who had, in fact, married a Porter.

Oftentimes bitter words were spoken when a Porter began to discuss a Putnam or vice versa. Her mother did not like for Mary to hear such things. She had even begun inventing errands for her when Goody Dawson came over with her tales of the possessed girls and how Sarah Good had bewitched her cow. But it was different with the Porters. She knew that her mother admired them, and she also knew that her mother shared many of their views about the Putnams. So it might be that her mother had some bitter things to say and did not want Mary to hear them.

Still, Mary did not like being left out, and she wanted to know what was being discussed. Somewhere between checking on the ewe and fetching the cider, Mary decided she would learn more about all of this, this bad blood between the Porters and the Putnams, and why the Putnams buttered the bread of the Reverend Lawson, a man she only dimly remembered.

Mary would have to bide her time, because there was no excuse she could invent today for going into the village; indeed, the entire village would be dedicated to fasting and praying. Her mother might let a fool like Gilly go, but not her own daughter. Besides, there was simply too much to do today with Gilly gone. And now the dream of a link between the Chase farm and the sea was coming closer to reality.

Mary was as excited about Daniel Andrews buying the Frost Fish Brook landing as her mother had been. She was determined to have an entire shallop loaded with Chase salt pork and gunny bags of flour. No more filling the tavern larders. Chase farm produce was destined for ship holds. That was where the money was to be made. So after Mary had checked on the ewe and had served more cider, she went out to check on the kichen garden. She had talked to her mother about doubling its size and devoting half of it to potatoes and other root vegetables. Captains of square rigs liked root vegetables. They weathered well.

CHAPTER
FIFTEEN

Gilly stood in the back of the meetinghouse. Between the prayers, when the congregation did not have to have their heads bowed and their eyes closed, Gilly craned his neck to try to glimpse the ministers who had come all the way from the North Shore.

Surely with the presence and the power of these great men who had traveled so far, the other two witches would be revealed. Gilly now strained to see the afflicted girls, who occupied seats of honor toward the front of the room. The prayers were mighty and stirred Gilly to the bottom of his soul. For these learned men were wrestling with Satan, the fallen angel of the Lord.

Again and again they prayed for help, for strength to penetrate the invisible realm in which the children were held hostage by the Devil's servants, his familiars. Who were they? Who were these vile people who had sold their souls to Lucifer?

Suddenly Ann Putnam junior jumped from her seat. "I see! I see! The other witch!"

Immediately her father and the Reverend Parris

were by her side. A knot of people tightened around her. A gasp rolled through the room. Why were they gasping? Gilly was puzzled. Had she named the witch? Was it another raving woman like Sarah Good, or one dark and strange with her island ways like Tituba? Or one like Sarah Osburne who had bedded with her servant before marrying him?

"Who is it?" Gilly turned to the man next to him.

"Martha Cory."

And soon the name reverberated through the meetinghouse. Martha Cory! A respected matron in good standing of the congregation. Unlike Sarah Osburne, she had never missed a meeting — except this one. Like Virginia, Martha Cory thought anything to do with witches and witchcraft was complete and utter nonsense.

The meeting came to a close. People rushed out the door and then lingered in dark clumps along the roadside. Gilly tried to listen, but he could only catch fragments of conversation. He did not feel comfortable enough to simply walk up to a group and join in the talk.

"They're going to need more than that," John Procter said vehemently. "She's a fine woman, a God-fearing woman. They'll not accuse her on the ravings of a child."

The group suddenly fell silent as Thomas Putnam

grimly approached. "All caution will be taken in this task. Fear not, John Procter. The Reverend Deodat Lawson comes soon."

"Deodat Lawson — and you feel he is truly an impartial observer, Thomas?"

"What do you mean by that, John?" A dark look passed between the men.

As Gilly walked by another group, he heard more. "There were mutterings all week about her," Goody Dawson said in an excited voice. "But my word, if it's true, just think of his power! That the Devil can make his way into the very heart of the church!"

"Into the soul of a covenanting member of the church." Thomas Putnam came up and spoke in a soft voice.

A hush fell upon the group, and Gilly moved away. His pace quickened. He could not wait to get back to the farm with his important news. Virginia would think this special, so special. He must remember the words exactly. He would repeat them as he went.

"This game has turned deadly now!" The color rose in Virginia's cheeks. Her eyes burned bright, almost feverish.

"And she is a covenanting member of the church, and then for the Devil to make his way."

"Hold your tongue, Gilly!" The words lashed out.

* * *

This was not going the way Gilly had imagined, and he had said it all correctly, he knew it. But Goodwife Chase was getting angrier and angrier.

"I shall not have this slander spoken."

And the angrier Goodwife Chase got, the more exciting she became to him. He wondered if the part of her legs that he was sometimes able to glimpse from his perch beneath the dormer ever turned as pink as the two spots on her cheeks.

"We shall have no further talk of this. There is work to be done, Gilly. I want to begin shearing next week. Go sharpen the shears. And we are doubling the kitchen garden. I want to put in a thousand of those seed potatoes. Mary has already sorted out the best. It looks like it will rain tonight. That will soften the ground. You should be prepared to do a first tilling on the new garden tomorrow."

It was obvious to Mary that her mother was doing precisely what John Procter had done when his servant girl, Mary Warren, had displayed signs of being afflicted: Set a piece of work to be done. For Mary Warren, it had been spinning. For Gilly, it was turning land and sharpening tools. But Mary herself felt torn. She wanted to hear more. It was unbelievable to her that Martha Cory had been named. If Martha Cory could be named, then could not . . . She did not finish the thought.

*   *   *

Two days later, as Mary helped Gilly turn soil in
the kitchen garden, she saw Goody Dawson's
wagon approaching. Oh dear, she thought, now
Mother is going to try to tell Goodwife Dawson to
hold her tongue. Perhaps before she did, Mary
would greet her down the way and gather some
more information as she walked beside the
Dawson's cart up the drive.

"Ah, it is a wicked business. But of course you
know, child, that there has been talk about Martha
Cory for some time now."

"There has?"

"Oh, yes." But Goody Dawson clamped her
mouth shut in a very uncharacteristic way. Mary
couldn't believe that the woman ever held back a
word in that tiny hole of a mouth between the two
puffy cheeks. But she was doing that right now.

"So what has happened?" Mary persisted.

"Deacon Edward Putnam and Ezekiel Cheever
went over to Martha's yesterday to examine her."

Mary and Goody Dawson had reached the
house, and Virginia had just come out the door,
wiping her hands on her apron.

"Good morrow, Goody Dawson. What brings
you here?"

"Are you shearing next week, Virginia?"

"We intend to."

"Could I bring the rams over, and could you do

94

them for me? Keep half the wool as payment. They are getting too rambunctious for my Benjamin." She patted her husband's knee. Benjamin Dawson rarely spoke, but he smiled now and said in a quiet voice, "If it is not too much trouble for your man Gilly."

"No, no, not at all," Virginia said. "Would you like to come in for a moment?"

"Of course." Goody Dawson was down from the cart in a flash.

"You heard about Martha Cory, no doubt?" she asked as they walked through the door.

"Yes, I have. Quite enough, I have heard," Virginia said pointedly. But Goody Dawson was oblivious and plowed on.

"Well, there'd been talk for some time."

She paused as if expecting Virginia to answer.

"Would you care for some cider, friends?"

"Ah, yes. I'll take some," Benjamin told her.

"Well," continued Goody Dawson, "as I was saying to your Mary outside, Deacon Edward Putnam and Ezekiel Cheever went over to Martha Cory's to examine her yesterday."

"They did, did they?" Virginia replied grimly.

"And do you know what she said when they told her that Ann Putnam had cried out upon her?" Goody Dawson waited briefly, but Virginia did not reply. Mary noticed that Benjamin, peering over the rim of his cider flagon, followed Virginia with watchful eyes. "Martha Cory said that she did not believe there were witches at all — just slothful persons, and one could not blame the Devil."

"I agree," said Virginia quietly.

But Goody Dawson had not heard her. "And then she asked the deacon and Goodman Cheever what clothes Ann Putnam said she had been wearing."

"Why would she ask a question like that?" Mary blurted out. Virginia gave her a sharp look.

"Oh, my dear, have you not heard that the afflicted girls can describe the clothes the witches wear?"

"No, ma'am."

"Well, it was of no use, anyway, because Ann Putnam said that when Martha Cory came to her, she blinded the poor girl so she could not see. The witches are becoming cleverer."

"Or perhaps the afflicted girls are becoming cleverer," Virginia said. "Oh, I nearly forgot. I have some soap set up out back and must go stir it."

"Time we are going ourselves," Benjamin Dawson said quietly. They rose to leave. "We shall be seeing you in meeting next Sunday? Deodat Lawson is to read the text."

"Of course. It has been so long since we have seen the Reverend Lawson." Her mother's voice sounded tight to Mary. As if the simplest words were struggling through some very small passage to get out. "I shall expect your rams next week.

We'll be shearing Monday and Tuesday and probably on into Wednesday."

Although her mother could hardly bear to talk of the witches, Mary's sense of urgency to find out all she could became stronger than ever. It was not merely a thirst for gossip. The affliction was spreading in new ways. If she could not fathom the mysteries of the invisible world with its specters and wizards and demons, then she must try to learn more about the visible one — the village, the Putnams and the Porters, and the bad blood between them.

And what was it that Goody Dawson — who always talked a streak — would not tell her about Martha Cory? Why had she so suddenly clamped her mouth shut?

If she understood some of these things, would it then be possible to get a sense of the strength of this invisible world's hold on people? Mary Chase was determined to go to the village tomorrow, no matter what.

CHAPTER
SIXTEEN

Mary Chase had met Mary Warren and Mary Walcott on the meetinghouse road outside the village, just as she was about to cross the bridge over Crane Brook. They were on their way to Ingersoll's Ordinary and had just returned from an errand for Ann Putnam senior. Mary Walcott sometimes lived with the Putnams as a servant girl. She, too, had been afflicted at about the same time that young Ann Putnam was first stricken. Mary Chase could not believe her good luck in running into the two Marys; certainly they, along with Ann Putnam, were at the center of the strange happenings. Mary Warren, however, was not so central, since her master would never let her attend the examinations.

"He is a good and decent man, John Procter," Mary Warren was saying.

"But he beat you!" said Mary Walcott.

"Yes, I know. He is confused and frustrated by all of this, and his wife — don't you know, she doesn't give him a moment's peace. He would have liked to have beaten her rather than me, I tell you."

Mary Chase gasped. "No, it can't be true, not with her being in the family way."

"She's expecting another?" asked Mary Walcott.

"Yes. The baby's just started, and let me tell you, it has put Elizabeth Procter in a vile mood. She doesn't understand her husband. Not a bit." Then Mary Warren bit her lip lightly as if to think about what she might or might not say next. "You know — " she said and dropped her voice to a whisper. The color rose in her cheeks. She began again. "You know what John Procter said to me?"

"What?" the other two Marys asked.

"Well, he says that I am the only one who truly understands him."

"And that's why he beats you?" Mary Chase asked.

Both girls gave her a chilling look. Had she said something wrong? There was something here that she was not understanding.

"Deodat Lawson is coming today, I believe. He will be at Ingersoll's," Mary Walcott said.

"I hardly remember the man," Mary Chase told her.

"Oh, he is very learned, indeed," Mary Walcott

said. "Goody Putnam says he is ever so much deeper than the Reverend Parris. She is quite fond of him. That is why I bring this four-grain cake for him. That woman keeps me running. First, all the way out to Potter Frederick at Hadlock's Bridge, and now back to Ingersoll's with this. It's a wonder I have a breath left by the day's end."

But Mary Chase was not thinking about Mary Walcott's running about. She was thinking about the four-grain cake the girl carried in her basket for Deodat Lawson, and she was remembering what Israel Porter had said about the Reverend Lawson knowing which side his bread was buttered on. Apparently they not only gave him the butter, but the bread to go with it.

"I daresay," Mary Walcott continued, "if you could have seen the poor lady last night."

"What poor lady?"

"Why, Goody Putnam. She was having fits herself. You haven't heard?"

"No. I thought it was just young Ann."

"Ah, no, Mary. Last night the familiar of Martha Cory came. Goody Putnam was all wearied out from tending her little afflicted one, when suddenly Goody Cory's shape appeared and tortured her so badly she could hardly express it. It was ready to tear her to bits. Mark my words, it was a terrible sight."

Mary Walcott's face did not match her tone. Not at all, Mary Chase observed. The rather round face with gentle contours had hardened into an inscrutable mask. There seemed to be no more sympathy in it for her mistress than in Mary Warren's when she talked about Elizabeth Procter. And then Mary had a strange thought. *We are three Marys, but how very different we are.* She could not put her finger on what made the difference, but she felt sure it was not because they were possessed and she was not. No, they seemed quite in control, and they seemed to know things she would never know.

It was nearing the end of the day. Despite all the errands she had run for her mistress, Mary Walcott did have breath — breath for one of the worst fits Mary Chase had witnessed yet.

They had entered the tavern of Nathaniel Ingersoll, and Mary Walcott had presented Ann Putnam's four-grain cake, when a bloodcurdling shriek curled from her mouth. "She bit me! She bit me!" Mary Walcott screamed and fell to the floor. She would have knocked her head on a stone jug had Ingersoll himself not caught her in time.

Mary Walcott writhed in pain on the floor for several minutes. Then, with her face smeared with tears, she called to the minister. "Come, Reverend Lawson, bring that candle. See for yourself."

Mary Chase and Mary Warren watched as the

Reverend Deodat Lawson crouched beside the panting figure.

"Yes. Yes, for sure I see some marks. Apparently teeth marks, both upper and lower set!" he said, lifting the girl's wrist.

Mary Walcott was helped to her feet, and Nathaniel Ingersoll sent John Indian for a cold cloth to put on her wrist.

"Can you help her home?" Nathaniel asked Mary Warren.

"Oh, yes, sir."

Mary Chase shrank back into the shadows of the tavern room. She studied the Reverend Deodat Lawson as he settled into a chair at a table near a window with his flagon of cider. He signaled John Indian. "A pot of ink and a quill," he said abruptly.

John Indian returned with the reverend's request. Lawson then drew out of his cloak a book and began writing. He was intent on his work. His skin was the color of tallow, and it glistened in the pale light that came through the leaded panes of the window. His eyelids fluttered with dim pulses. He gripped the quill tightly. He seemed excited to the point of agitation as he wrote.

In the meantime, Nathaniel Ingersoll was speaking in his booming voice to two travelers from Boston who had arrived just at the finish of Mary Walcott's fit.

"I apologize," he said to the man and woman. "You've no doubt heard about the troubles here in our village. The poor afflicted girls." At that moment, John Indian came with their cider, and Ingersoll left.

"Did he tell you about the witches?" John Indian asked, his eyes gleaming.

"Witches, you say? There is witchcraft here in Salem Village?" the woman asked.

"Oh, absolutely, ma'am. I'll show you. They bite me something fierce."

Mary could hardly believe her ears or her eyes. John Indian, usually so docile, was now speaking quite animatedly and unbuttoning his shirt. In a graceful turn, he wheeled about and showed his bare back to the two strangers. "These are the scars they make on my back."

To Mary they looked like old scars, and she wondered why John Indian was doing this. His own wife, Tituba, had been arrested, and now she languished in jail. What possible good could all this talk do?

Then Deodat Lawson beckoned him over to his table. He rose and carefully examined the scars on John Indian's back, and went back to his writing.

Mary was stunned by the events of the last few minutes. She reflected on all that she had seen and heard. Why, even Nathaniel Ingersoll himself seemed to take Mary Walcott's fit in stride. Was the whole village afflicted in some strange way?

She would tell Caleb about it when he came. He had promised he would be at Ingersoll's before sunset. When she had left the farm that morning, she had told her mother that she was going to Salem Town to visit Caleb and spend the day; that her mother need not worry, for Caleb would walk her home and stay the night so as to attend meeting the next day.

She had done almost that. She had left at dawn for Salem Town. And indeed, when she got there, Caleb had said he would accompany her home. But she had not planned to spend the rest of the day in town but rather in the Village of Salem to find out more.

Caleb had been as shocked as she about the charges brought against Martha Cory. The image of Abigail Williams's contorted face and the twisted faces of the other girls had never entirely left his mind. When Mary had told him about Martha Cory, a deep fear welled up inside him. He knew that Mary was right. They must learn as much as possible about the strange affliction and its increasing hold on the girls and the people of Salem Village. He had agreed to leave work early, for he had put in extra time all week. He would meet Mary at Ingersoll's. From there they would walk home together. Now Mary waited patiently for him.

Thomas Putnam strode in through the door. Lawson quickly rose, and the men greeted each other warmly.

"Come, come right over. My dear wife is near exhaustion from tending the girls. But she is, of course, anxious to see you, dear friend."

"Yes, and a most grievous episode did I witness minutes before with Mary Walcott."

"I heard! I heard. The child is home now, safe for the moment. We must go to the parsonage." There was a bright, eager look on Thomas Putnam's face.

The men had not been gone for five minutes when Caleb arrived. Mary was out of her seat practically before her brother was through the door. The day was darkening as the sun rapidly sank.

"Caleb, we must go to that lilac bush you told me of this morning, the one by the parsonage."

As they walked, Mary explained what she had seen and heard that day, ever since she had met the two Marys on the Crane Brook bridge.

"Mary Warren, I would not worry about. She is a flighty thing," Caleb was saying. "But Mary Walcott is not. She is steady and thoughtful. She is living with the Putnams?"

"Yes. Her stepmother, Deliverance, has four or more little ones now, and her father, Jonathan, is a brother-in-law of Thomas Putnam. So sometimes Mary does stay there. She says it's really a rest to get away from all the babies."

By the time they turned down the lane to the parsonage, dusk had settled thickly on the land. They moved quietly through the deepening shadows to the lilac bush. Inside the house they could see the glow of several candles and kerosene lamps. There was some commotion in the room. A figure streaked by the window. They crouched just under the sill.

"Whish! Whish," they heard a voice squealing.

"It's Abigail," Caleb said. "Worse than before. Look at her flapping her arms." Mary pressed her face closer. She saw Deodat Lawson watching the spectacle, his writing book clutched to his breast. Thomas Putnam and the Reverend Parris tried to subdue the child. They were moving toward a bench near the fire.

"I won't, I won't!" she screamed.

"Won't what?" cried her aunt Elizabeth, who, in utter anguish, was tearing at her own face with her fingers.

"Do you not see her? She stands there! I won't sign the book! I am sure it is none of God's book. It's the Devil's book, for all I know. I won't, I won't."

106

They had finally wrestled her into a chair. Suddenly she was quiet. Her body went limp. She stared into nothingness like a blind person.

"Abigail! Abigail!" her uncle, the Reverend Parris, shouted repeatedly. But she did not seem to hear him.

"What's happening to her face?" Mary asked in horror as she watched the girl's jaw go slack and then seem to slip out of joint.

The girl's tongue lolled out, long as an eel. Her eyes widened. She began making the most piteous cries. "Do you not see her?" she cried, and then she jumped up.

It happened so suddenly that Mary and Caleb could not follow the girl's flight across the room, but in one swift moment she had leaped into the hearth and had come back swinging firebrands. She began hurling them about the house. Then she raced back to the fireplace.

"She's trying to climb up the chimney," Mary gasped. But the girl's uncle and the Reverend Lawson pulled her back just in time.

"The specter is here in the room. She draws me up the chimney."

"Who? Who?" came the cries.

" 'Tis Goody Nurse. Rebecca Nurse." The girl said the name loud and clear.

Mary and Caleb looked at each other in horror. The second witch had been named. First Martha

Cory, and now Rebecca Nurse, two of the most pious and respected members of the congregation.

"If they are witches," Caleb said, his breath hot on Mary's cheek, "then we'll all be witches by spring!"

CHAPTER
SEVENTEEN

A rogue's moon rode high in the sky, hiding behind shreds of torn clouds. Mary and Caleb walked in silence. What they had seen was unbelievable. Abigail Williams had been in the grip of some powerful force. Mary touched her jaw softly and remembered the terrible way in which Abigail's had sprung out, her tongue stretching into a long, disgusting, shimmering shape. It was as if an eel had uncoiled from deep within her throat. But despite these horrors, there was another image that was not horrible at all; it lurked at the back of her mind. In the midst of all the commotion and the screeching and the flinging of firebrands, there had been something else, and now she could not remember it. But it had seemed important at the time. Perhaps she would think of it later. Tomorrow they would all go to meeting together. They would hear the Reverend Lawson.

Mary had been so lost in her thoughts, she had not realized that they were almost upon their own house. She was startled when Caleb suddenly grabbed her forearm.

"Hush! We have a prowler!" he whispered.

"What?"

Caleb put his finger to his lips and then pointed to the space above the calving shed roof. There indeed was a figure crouched beneath the dormer of their mother's room.

The ritual had become familiar to Gilly. First she untied her cap and set it down on the table. Then she pulled something from her hair, gave her head a bit of a shake, and Gilly watched as a cascade of pale fire fell down her back.

Next, Virginia undid the wings that covered the shoulders of her dress. Then she slipped off the sleeves that detached from the bodice and then the bodice itself. She would stand sometimes for several seconds before she took off her overskirt. Still in her underskirt, she would busy herself in the room, putting the garments she had just taken off onto their proper pegs or in the drawers. After this, she would remove her underskirt and stand in her thin chemise. She would then reach inside the chemise and loosen something. The underdrawers dropped to the floor. If she stood at just the right angle to the kerosene lamp, its light limned the shape of her body, and Gilly could see it perfectly through the thin material of the chemise. She would bend over in a gesture as smooth as a blue heron in the marsh, and he would see the soft shadows of her thighs.

But suddenly he heard her yelp. She wheeled about. The last things he remembered were her gray eyes like twin silvery moons looming out of a storm-torn night — bright and harsh and full of fear. Then Gilly felt something tighten around his chest, and he was rolling, rolling, rolling.

They fell together onto a heap of straw bales. Powerful hands tightened around his throat.

The voices sounded dim and far away. "You'll kill him! You'll kill him! Stop it, Caleb." The world had begun to blacken. And then, finally, a bubble of air. He could breathe.

"You dog! You dog! What were you doing?" Caleb was shouting at him and shaking him. He looked up. Virginia and Mary were standing over him. Virginia Chase's face was like a death mask. The eyes were hollow and lifeless. Mary Chase stood trembling. She held a pitchfork poised above his chest.

They spoke so fast. He could hardly follow what they were saying. They were angry, terribly angry with him. And now Virginia was screaming, "Why? Why, Gilly?" And in the dimness of his brain, he began to understand what they wanted to know.

"But Goody Chase," he said in a low, croaking

voice. He rubbed his throat as if to coax the words out. "I ain't never seen a woman's legs before. I wanted to see your legs."

"You are an abomination, Gilly Beales!" And with that, Virginia Chase spat on him.

"Off! Off! Off our land," Caleb shouted.

CHAPTER
EIGHTEEN

The Chases arrived early at the meetinghouse for the Sunday service. They took their customary seats. Mary could hardly believe that the deformed and raging Abigail Williams of the night before now entered the meetinghouse, rosy and cheerful, holding her aunt's hand.

Could this be the same girl whose jaw had appeared to slip from its hinge the night before, whose tongue had protruded as long and writhing as a slippery eel? Next, Mercy Lewis entered with Ann Putnam and her mother, Ann Putnam senior, and then Mary Walcott. The eyes of the congregation followed the path of the afflicted girls as they made their way to their seats. The girls themselves cast their eyes down — not in shame, but with modesty, a modesty that befitted the position of distinguished guests who wore their honor with ease. These girls had become august presences.

The congregation was clearly in awe of them; their attention was so wholly focused on the girls that the Reverend Deodat Lawson entered the meetinghouse unnoticed. The minister walked up to the pulpit. His hollow eyes scanned the congregation. There was a sudden flicker of astonishment, and then the entire congregation gasped as Martha Cory walked through the door and took her usual seat.

How dare an accused witch show herself in this Godly place on the eve of her examination?

The congregation's attention focused on Goodwife Cory, who was sitting quietly with her hands folded in her lap over *The Book of Common Prayer.* Her defiance was an abomination. The very odor of it seeped through the congregation like poison. One by one the girls began to tremble.

"Now stand up and name your text," Abigail Williams shouted. She jumped to her feet and pointed an accusatory finger at the Reverend Lawson.

There were more gasps from the congregation. The child must have been possessed to be confronting God's minister like this. This was not mere childish impudence. This was the Devil, curled like a worm in the bosom of the church.

The other girls began to wail. The reverend could scarcely speak his sermon. But he was not angered by these disruptions, for each time he looked with awe and sympathy upon the afflicted girls.

"Look!" cried Abigail. "Goody Cory's bird. Her yellow bird!"

Then Ann Putnam junior looked toward the rafters, where Abigail had pointed. "It suckles with Goody Cory's shape on the beam over there!"

And although Goody Cory's ample and comfortable figure sat on the bench, every eye in the congregation shifted to the ceiling beam, expecting to see Goody Cory's shape.

"Ah, there it flutters," said Ann Putnam, "to the minister's hat, hanging on the pulpit."

Again the congregation's eyes shifted to where Deodat Lawson's hat hung. Lawson himself took two steps back from the pulpit. But he continued to read from his text: *"Have I not chosen you twelve and one of you is the Devil?"*

When he had finished reading the scripture, the Reverend Lawson continued with his sermon:

"So far as we can look into those hellish mysteries and guess at the administration of that kingdom of darkness, we may learn that witches make witches by persuading one another to subscribe to a book or articles, and the Devil . . . will use their bodies and minds and shapes . . . to affright and afflict others at his pleasure. . . ."

Then Mary and Caleb heard a calm, soft voice. "Come, children. We must leave." Virginia rose abruptly and walked down the aisle of the meetinghouse. She went out the door and slammed it behind her. Just before they walked through the door, Mary had turned her head slightly to the side.

She saw Thomas Putnam's face. He was quite calm. There were the bare traces of a smile etched in his jaw, and in his eyes was a glint of triumph.

It was in this fleeting moment that Mary remembered what it was she had tried to recall the night before — the image that had lurked like a shadow amidst the dark horrors of Abigail's fit. It had been just this: Thomas Putnam's smile. He was pleased. He had been pleased by the fits of his daughter and Abigail the night before, and he was pleased that Virginia Chase and her children were now walking out of the meetinghouse.

CHAPTER
NINETEEN

G oody Dawson scowled as she watched
Virginia and Mary wrestling with the ram.
Virginia seemed uncommonly strong to her, even
if she had been widowed these past two years
and had to do more than a woman's share of the
heavy work.

It was too bad Gilly had left. Virginia had offered
no explanation. But the result was that Virginia
and Mary, who was just a spindly thing, were left
to deal with the two rams Goody Dawson and her
husband had brought over. And now, come to think
of it, look at that Mary — for a spindly thing, she
surely had a good clamp on that ram's forelegs as
she began to shear.

"You're patchin' him?" cried Goody Dawson.

"Just a small nick, Goody," answered Mary as
she took some wool soaked in liniment from a
pocket and pressed it to the ram's shoulder to stop
the bleeding.

"You see where she nicks them, Benjamin."
Goody Dawson turned to her husband. In a low

voice she added, "Same place each time — inside the shoulder close to the heart."

"Never you mind. They're doing a reputable job."

But the scowl lines in Goody Dawson's brow deepened.

A few minutes later, Virginia stood with the wool in her arms. This was her payment for shearing the rams, and she watched as the Dawson's cart made its way down the lane toward the road.

"Goody Dawson barely thanked you, Mother."

"I know."

Mary looked at her mother. There was a little pulse near where her jaw met her neck, which often throbbed when Virginia was upset or nervous. In the bright sunlight it seemed to be jumping madly in some insane rhythm. Mary felt her own heart beating at a jittery, quick pace. She dared not look down at her own bodice for fear of seeing the plain muslin suddenly jumping about. But the last few days had been enough to tear a heart from a soul.

It had all happened so fast. On the Monday after the Reverend Deodat Lawson's meeting, Martha Cory had been examined and officially charged with witchcraft. They had hauled her off to prison to join Tituba and Sarah Good and Sarah Osburne. By that evening, rumors swirled that Rebecca Nurse would be charged.

When Goody Dawson had arrived at the Chase Farm with her two rams, she had been full of the story. "It's not mere pinching and tweaking this time, Goody Chase." The words had popped out of her mouth like little punching fists. "Oh, no. It is more than that this time with Rebecca Nurse, they say."

"Says who?" Virginia had asked.

"Says Ann Putnam senior." Goody Dawson had nodded firmly.

"But Goody Dawson, you know how frail of mind Ann Putnam senior is. She has never recovered from losing her little ones."

"That's just the point," Goody Dawson had said, her small eyes growing round as coins.

"What is the point?"

"They were murdered, those infants!"

"Murdered!" Virginia and Mary had both gasped.

"Yes, indeed. Little children began appearing to Ann Putnam senior in winding sheets. Some called her Mother, some called her Aunt — they were the ones of her sister, and they all said the same thing. It was Rebecca Nurse who killed them, in cold blood."

"I shan't hear another word of it. If you want these rams sheared, you must mind your tongue."

Mary was shocked. She had never heard her mother speak so sharply. Then Benjamin Dawson did a rare thing — he spoke up. "Be still, Wife. It is a mistake with Rebecca Nurse. I am sure of that. No finer, more pious woman ever was."

"Yes, Benjamin," whispered Virginia.

But Goody Dawson had given her husband a fearsome stare, and if it were not for the fact that she wanted to spare the old man's back, Mary had no doubt that Goody Dawson would have taken the rams away right then.

Mary wondered if Goody Dawson could hold her tongue long enough even to get to the Ipswich Road, let alone home, before lashing out at her husband.

Well, she did not have time to wonder. Today was the day she was making a delivery to Daniel Andrews at the Frost Fish Brook dock. Mary would go along with the pork, the whole grain, and the flour from the Chase farm that would be floated down to Salem Town to sell to the ships. For Daniel Andrews had invited her to come for the ride. "After all, you cannot weigh much more than a bag of cornmeal." She could ride atop the cargo, have a visit with her brother, then return with Daniel upstream that evening and be welcomed to pass the night with him and his wife, Sarah, the daughter of John Porter. Mary had been looking forward to this day for a long time, and now she vowed nothing would spoil it, not even Goody Dawson.

* * *

She was ferociously hungry from having spent the morning shearing and was most eager to get on her way, but she did wait long enough for her mother to pack a lunch pail. As hard as it had been since Gilly had left, this was one piece of extra work that she would enjoy doing. It made her feel important to be taking these goods all by herself for delivery to Salem Town. They loaded the cart and hitched up the horses. Mary kissed her mother good-bye.

"Don't worry. I'll be back by suppertime tomorrow," she said and slapped the reins on Sweet Sass's hind. The big draft horse began to walk slowly down the lane.

There was a secret life to the countryside, and if one was of keen eye and a still nature, it revealed itself — a rapid wing beat, a flash of color, a glimpse of a vanishing tail under a bush. It was this hidden life beneath the familiar patterns that caught Mary's interest whenever she was out alone and abroad in the countryside. She looked for it now as she drove the cart toward the village.

Overhead she spotted a kestrel hovering in mid-flight, its head to the wind, hunting, no doubt. Then, just seconds later, at the edge of the road, under a thick hummock of grass, she spied the quivering whiskers of a vole. The whiskers blended perfectly with the dun-colored grass. The only difference was that the grass, shivered by a gentle wind, moved at a different rhythm from the trembling whiskers of the vole. There was no need for Mary to warn the creature that its archenemy flew overhead. The vole was aware. She could tell, for it did not even nibble the fat tuber it held between its paws; it remained still, except for its whiskers.

The little animal must be far from its hole, she thought. But the fields were crisscrossed with an endless network of tunnels and runs, so the tiny creatures could escape the kestrel and any other menace from above. It occurred to Mary that there were as many runs and tunnels in this one field as there were creeks and streams in the surrounding countryside.

She thought now about those streams that she and Caleb had played in so often when they were younger, wading and catching crayfish, sailing little twig boats with leaves for mainsails. The creeks and brooks were like a liquid spiderweb cast upon the land. Follow one, and it opened to another, then perhaps broadened to a river that flowed toward the sea. Sometimes they just dwindled off into marshes and bogs. The banks often shifted, the course of the water changed, the bottom of a creek might silt up, and what was navigable one year might be too shallow to wade the next. Ten years ago, she had heard Israel Porter say, the Frost Fish Brook would not have been deep enough for

Daniel Andrews's enterprise. But now it was. Mary wondered if the courses of the vole, its tunnels and runways, shifted like those of the brook.

She arrived at the Frost Fish Brook before she knew it, and Daniel was there, standing on the pier. Other farmers had already arrived, so Mary's bags of flour and wheat and salt pork were the last to be loaded.

"Are you going to meeting this Thursday, Daniel? It's the Reverend Lawson again. The Lecture Day sermon."

"Oh, I think I got my fill Sunday last."

"Aye, I would agree with that myself," said Goodman Barnes.

John Procter, who stood near, added, "They should be at the whipping post, those girls. I said it last night, and I'll say it again: If they are let alone, we shall all be devils and witches."

"Now, don't you go saying that in the village, John Procter," Daniel Andrews warned.

"Yes, but he is right," said another.

"And I certainly have had enough of the Reverends Parris and Lawson," Daniel Andrews added, then muttered under his breath, "If they are really going after Rebecca Nurse, the Porters will make sure there will be hell to pay."

The men's words were a comfort to Mary. It had been so long since she had heard people speak with reason, particularly groups of people. She remembered how, in meeting the previous Sunday, when the girls had cried out about Martha Cory's yellow bird, grown men and women had actually looked up, turning their eyes to the rafters as if reason had totally left them — and they actually expected to see a bird, the spirit of Martha Cory, sitting up there.

But these men here today were only four. And how many had there been at the meeting? Twenty? Thirty or more? In any case, there was perhaps a tiny shred of hope in hearing men speak this way.

Mary sat high on a pile of burlap bags as the shallop floated down the stream. The boat had a flat bottom and a sail, but Daniel Andrews could not raise the sail until the course of the brook turned northeast so the southwestern wind could fill the sail. In the meantime, he and another man poled on either side.

Sometimes the banks were so close that Mary could reach out and touch an overhanging branch. The frogs had not yet awakened, but in another month their eggs — like clear glass beads — would be floating in clusters in the water.

Suddenly Mary saw the water fold like draped cloth. A beaver's snout broke through the surface. In the trees and scrubby brush that lined the banks was a stain of green. Buds had begun to swell, and who knew what mysterious pushings were going on beneath the ground. Spring was really coming.

Blossoms would break from their tight sheaths, tadpoles would burst from their glassy orbs, and within the course of weeks, the tadpoles would lose their tails, grow legs, and become frogs. The air would hum with the song of insects, and branches would be festooned with the glistening webs of spiders, a finery that would put even the best lacework to shame.

Caleb had told Mary that spider legs were coated with oil so the weaver would never get caught in its own web. How clever of God to make a spider that way, Mary suddenly thought. But then another thought struck her with greater force. What kind of clever God would make Ann Putnam?

Mary could feel the color drain from her face. She had never questioned God in this way. It frightened her terribly. But one minute she had been thinking about spiderwebs with insects tangled at their centers, and the next minute the spiderweb dissolved. Instead of insects and glistening threads, there were dead babies in winding sheets. A wisp of hair from under her cap blew across her face.

"We're round the bend, and the wind is aft," Daniel Andrews called out cheerfully. "Want to help me raise the sail, Mary?"

The brook had been gradually broadening, and now it turned and expanded as the waters of the Frost Fish Brook joined those of the Crane River, and together they flowed into the Wooleston. Mary scrambled down from the pile of cargo and stood near Daniel Andrews.

"You haul, Mary, and I'll be at the tiller. When she gets to the top, you cleat her down firm now. If she's too heavy for you when the wind punches into the full sail, call Martin. He'll give you a hand."

Mary couldn't believe it. In the space of one day she had been trusted to get all these goods from their farm to Salem Town, and now Daniel Andrews had asked her to haul the sail as if she were some old salt.

The wind had freshened, and she could feel it press into the canvas. The sail was barely a quarter of the way up. She hoped she would be able to haul it all the way and not have to call for Martin's help.

"You're doin' a fine job, Mary," Daniel called out.

The sail suddenly seemed to come alive in her hands with a feisty will of its own. She pulled harder, putting her whole back into the job, biting down on her lip as she concentrated. It was Mary's belief that concentration could almost make up for anything she lacked in muscle. She remembered the old ram of Goody Dawson's she and her mother had wrestled that morning. If she could handle the ram, she could handle this sail.

"You're at the top, lass!" Daniel cried out. "Now cleat her."

The shallop suddenly sprang ahead. She was a sprightly thing dancing across the water. Riverbanks slipped by. Mary had a firm hold on the hauling rope, but the boat heeled a bit to one side. She had to brace her foot against a side of pork, then lean her shoulder into the mast. She twisted the rope into a figure eight onto the cleat, and then she clamped the tail of the rope securely under the bottom loop as Caleb had shown her.

"Well, I declare, Mary Chase. You'll be commanding your own rig in the China Seas before you know it." Daniel Andrews laughed and threw back his head. The wind whipped his dark blond hair until his entire head looked like a flaring, radiant sun. He was a bold and merry man. She remembered her father saying that Daniel Andrews could brighten the darkest winter day with his ready smile and generous heart.

CHAPTER
TWENTY

"Oh, can I try, Caleb? Try sanding that cleat piece there? Did I tell you that Daniel Andrews let me raise the sail, and then I had to cleat the rope?"

"Sheet, Mary. They call them sheets on boats, not ropes."

"Well, no matter. I cleated the sheet for him. And there was a full breeze in the sail, but the cleat was much smaller than this one here."

The one Caleb had in the vise on the workbench was almost a foot long.

"Well, this is for a full-rigged ship, Mary, and not a shallop."

"True."

"But tell me this news about Rebecca Nurse."

"I already told you."

Caleb sat back and watched his sister as she rubbed the sanding block over the cleat. He had repeatedly tried to get her to tell him about Rebecca Nurse, but each time he asked, she interrupted his questions with one more detail about her sail down the Frost Fish Brook — how Daniel Andrews had let her do this, how Daniel Andrews had let her do that. When the shallop arrived at the wharves in Salem Town, Daniel had let her hand off the lines, then jump off and tie the stern.

Clearly, Mary did not want to talk about the trouble in the village, but more and more people in Salem Town were talking about it, and this worried Caleb. Should he be so worried?

He did not want to unnecessarily alarm his mother and sister. But ever since the awful business with Gilly, Caleb had been nervous. He was not that far away, but in some ways, he might as well have been in China. It was harder when one was away from family. You always imagined the worst. But on the other hand, had they simply become accustomed to the strangeness? Did it no longer seem strange to them?

But how could it not? This news about Rebecca Nurse was terrible. The Porters of Salem Town were buzzing about it, for they were close to both Rebecca and Francis Nurse.

He would try another question. "Mary, Daniel Andrews — he is married to Sarah Porter. Was he not upset about Rebecca Nurse?"

"Well, I'm sure. And I did hear him say that he has had enough of the Reverends Lawson and Parris, and — " Mary paused. "Yes, and then he said something about 'if they are going after Goody Nurse, the Porters will make sure there will be hell to pay.' "

Caleb inhaled sharply. So many thoughts pressed on his brain, thoughts he did not even want to think himself, let alone utter to his younger sister. But he vowed to put in double shifts these next weeks to earn extra time off. He was sure Master Jeremy would understand.

When his sister left, Caleb pushed the thoughts of Salem Village from his mind. Worried as he was, he knew that a wandering mind could make mistakes. One slip of an adze, and a finger could be lost. Even when sanding, one could lose the course of the grain if one's mind wandered from the wood and the sound of the sanding block's tone. But when he had cleaned and hung up his tools for the evening, had his cider and bowl of stew, his mind returned to the problems of Salem Village.

As Caleb lay on his pallet that night in the tiny shed room off the finishing shop, he thought about Sarah Osburne and now Martha Cory and Rebecca Nurse. Was there not a pattern here? For sure, Sarah Good and Tituba did not fit it. But were not these other women full-fledged church members and the wives of well-to-do freeholders? Most significantly, however, Martha Cory and Rebecca and Francis Nurse were friends of the Porters, and the Porters had opposed the appointment of Samuel Parris. The Putnams had not.

130

Caleb could not remember a time when the Porters and the Putnams had not been rivals. They were the two richest families in the area, but recently the Putnam fortunes had taken a turn for the worse. The Porters were more enterprising, more willing to attempt bold ventures. They held much more land in Salem Town, which was becoming the most prosperous place in the entire colony with its shipping. But Caleb knew that Parris and the Putnams thought Salem Town was becoming too worldly, too Godless; the town, they felt, was turning away from the old Puritan ways and rules of the church to pursue a worldwide commerce.

Was all this witch business somehow mixed up with the age-old rivalry between the families? Could it all come down to money?

People, after all, were nervous now. The Commonwealth had been without a charter for too long. The king had revoked the charter when he had become angry with the colonies back in 1684. The charter, as Caleb understood it, provided the means for governing legally; through the charter, land titles had been granted. And without a charter, these titles — and people's very property — became vulnerable. In fact, Caleb thought, without a charter, the Commonwealth was at the mercy of the most lawless forces, like a ship without a rudder. No wonder people were frightened and scrambling for all they could get, and resentful of what they had already lost.

Now that Caleb thought of it, there were two patterns. First, the accused witches were all of families that had increased their holdings and become richer and more respected by the community in recent years; and second, at least in the case of Rebecca Nurse, her house was closer to the town than the village. The most vigorous accusers came from the center of the village. Now would the orbit of the accusers expand eastward? And would other witches be found closer and closer to Salem Town? That would perhaps be the only way they could ever get to the Porters without actually accusing a Porter. For the Porter holdings were mostly east of the village, on the border between the village and the town, or in Salem Town itself.

Although Caleb was unable to brush away the disturbing thoughts of Salem Village, the same was not true of his sister. Mary Chase had spent the evening in the warm company of Daniel Andrews and his wife, Sarah — the perfect finish to a perfect day. She had not allowed one thought of the hysterical girls and the village troubles to cross her mind. And Sarah and Daniel Andrews had made a point of not mentioning their deep concern for Rebecca Nurse. They felt that none of the recent goings-on made for civilized conversation, particularly in the presence of a child.

Mary had left the Andrews house immediately

after breakfast, and she had not been on the Ipswich Road five minutes when she spotted Constable Braybrook's wagon coming toward her. Her heart gave a lurch. The last time she had seen this wagon, it had carried Tituba and Sarah Good and Sarah Osburne to prison. Would she now see Rebecca Nurse in manacles being transported?

All the troubles rushed back. What a fool she had been to forget, or even to think she could forget the strangeness. From this distance, she could not spot anyone in the constable's wagon save Braybrook himself. It must be empty.

Mary felt a small riffle of relief blow through her. But just then, she did see something. It was a small head, barely big enough to peer over the sideboards. The two wagons were now just yards apart, less than forty feet. Mary slapped the reins on Sweet Sass's back. The old horse sped up. Then Mary called *whoa* as they drew alongside the constable's wagon.

Mary blinked in disbelief. It was little Dorcas Good, the daughter of Sarah Good, her tiny wrists and legs in manacles and chains. Constable Braybrook had stopped the cart.

"What are you doing with Dorcas?" Mary's face swam with confusion.

"Aye, it's a sad business. Constable Willard himself did not have the stomach for it. He is taking so many in these days, he gave the job to me."

"But Dorcas? Why Dorcas?"

"She's been tormentin' the girls, ever since her mother was arrested."

"Tormenting them! But how, Dorcas?" Mary asked, aghast. The child did not speak. Instead, she looked down at her dirty hands. They were clenched into tight fists.

"You want to tell her, child? Or should I?" the constable said in a low voice. The little girl continued to study her hands and the iron bands that held them, but she said nothing.

"Her shape's been running round the country like a little mad dog, biting the girls something fierce. The girls have the teeth marks to prove it."

"Are they a dog's? Or a child's?" Mary asked, somewhat sharply.

Constable Braybrook's eyes widened at the pert tone of this young lady. But in truth it was a question that he had never thought of, and now he wondered himself.

"It was her shape that did it, they say. I know not."

"Her shape!" Mary exclaimed. "But she is only a child of four."

Dorcas's little voice suddenly piped up. "Yes, and I am going all the way to Boston to join my mother," she chirped with a bright eagerness. "And the constable says when we get to Noddle's Island, we ride a ferry boat."

"Yes, child, that you will. Ride the big ferry boat," Constable Braybrook chortled.

Mary felt her stomach turn. Who was worse — the crazed girls who were the child's accusers, or this constable, who made a game out of transporting a four-year-old girl to prison?

CHAPTER
TWENTY-ONE

Deodat Lawson sat in his room at Ingersoll's Ordinary. He was writing not in his journal, as he had for the past several days, but on pieces of paper. He was composing the Lecture Day sermon he was to deliver that afternoon.

Lawson had only stayed for the preliminaries of Rebecca Nurse's examination. Now, as he wrote his sermon, it was going on in the meetinghouse. He had little doubt of the outcome. It was indeed amazing, the vessels that the Devil chose; this frail creature of seeming grace had become the Devil's most potent channel. And that, perhaps, would be the text of his sermon. For the village quaked now with a confounding mixture of awe and fear that women as pious as Rebecca Nurse and Martha Cory — women of great respectability, wives of prosperous landholders — could indeed become instruments of Satan.

But that was the cunningness of it all. He would remind the congregation that it was this cunning nature that allowed the Devil to worm his way into the hearts of professed believers, children of God.

Without them, the diabolic purpose of Satan's existence could not be attained.

So the reverend wrote on in his spidery hand. "It is certain that he never works more like the Prince of Darkness than when he looks most like an angel of light."

Deodat Lawson paused and whispered the words he had just written. They had a certain grace to them, and they were the truth. He was sure of it. For who better was the embodiment of an angel of light than dear old Rebecca Nurse — the perfect instrument for Satan. And as if to affirm the reverend's brilliant deduction, shrill cries began to tear through the air. So searing were the afflicted girls' screams that he could hear them at this distance across the road from the meeting-house.

He turned now to his journal and jotted down a note describing the hideous shrieks that came hurtling through the damp March air. He then quickly returned to his sermon. Indeed, it was shaping up into something quite excellent, if he did say so himself. He would open the sermon with the thundering text of Zechariah, which would draw the desired effect and set the tone.

And the Lord said unto Satan, the Lord rebuke thee, O Satan. Even the Lord that hath chosen Jerusalem rebuke thee. Is this not a brand plucked from the burning?

* * *

Deodat Lawson gloated over the parallels he would develop between Jerusalem and Salem, truly an inspired touch. For was not Salem — once a city in the wilderness — the new Jerusalem? And as it turned its eyes toward the temptations of trade and commerce and Mammon, had it not become a harlot on their own New England shores?

All week, Thomas and Edward Putnam had talked about the ills and sins of that city — a city guided by the Porters. What he'd heard had been evidence enough, as far as the good reverend was concerned. Had he known this before, when he himself had been the minister to this flock a few short years ago, he might not have ever left. Even now, however, despite no longer being the official minister of the village church, there was the possibility that he might become to Salem what Cotton Mather was becoming in Boston.

Suddenly an idea struck him with such force that he put down his pen and rose from the desk. His normally sallow complexion glowed.

He took the paper on which he had been writing and walked closer to the window where the light was better. He reread his words. They were stirring. They could move men's souls. If the Reverend Mather could do it, why not he?

Why not begin to publish? And not just this sermon, but perhaps all the notes he had been com-

138

piling in his journal. He, Deodat Lawson, would write a brief and true narrative of the witchcraft in Salem Village. For indeed he had become an eyewitness to some of the truly strange and remarkable events that were afflicting the innocents. Why, only last night he had been at the Putnams', and he had witnessed Ann Putnam senior lying on her bed in a strange, transfixed state.

He got up and walked back to the table where his journal lay. He read the passage: "I found her lying on the bed, having a sore fit. . . . Her husband had gone to her and found her so stiff that she could hardly bend down to pray. . . . She began to strive violently with her arms and legs; she then began to complain of and, as it were, converse personally with Goodwife Nurse, saying, 'Goodwife Nurse, be gone! . . . Are you not ashamed, a woman of your profession, to afflict a poor creature so? What hurt did I ever do you in my life?' "

Deodat Lawson looked up from the page and tapped his temple. It was good, quite good. He particularly liked his descriptions of Ann Putnam's stiff body, how she could not be bent for prayer.

But there was something lacking. Perhaps he needed to introduce himself more directly as an eyewitness. Perhaps he should say that she spoke to him, a bit earlier than she actually had, and that she was glad to see him, and then she fell down.

She had, after all, nodded in a friendly way toward him just before the worst of the fit. She had even said. . . .

No, he supposed Thomas Putnam had been the one to tell him that his wife had wanted him to come so they could pray together to chase the shape of Goody Nurse away. But did they really matter, these small details? Who was to know? It would make much better reading if he wrote that Ann Putnam herself, earlier on, had asked that he be right there to pray with her.

Deodat Lawson stretched his arms up in the air, wriggled his back a bit to get the kinks out. He felt enormously refreshed by the very thought of the task he had set before himself. That print-hungry Cotton Mather was not the only one who could turn a phrase. And Deodat Lawson knew this: He had better hurry up, because before he knew it, Mather would be making his way to Salem.

As Caleb Chase walked briskly into the village, he was surprised by the festive atmosphere. It was, after all, the day of the Lecture Day sermon, one of the most solemn events of the New England church year. The Reverend Deodat Lawson had been invited. Yet here, less than two hours before the sermon was to begin in the meetinghouse, villagers had spread out picnic lunches in the Parris's pasture and on the green in front of Ingersoll's Ordinary.

Indeed, the tavern itself was filled to the brim with people gossiping over cider and cakes. Ingersoll appeared to be extremely cheerful, and as the genial host, he greeted folks in the highest of spirits. There was an eerie, unreal atmosphere to the place.

Caleb made his way toward Ingersoll to ask him if what he had just heard outside was true about Goody Nurse: that minutes ago, the old lady had been put into Constable Willard's wagon and driven off to the Salem prison.

Nathaniel Ingersoll's dark brows knotted together. The deep lines of his face suddenly reflected a grave demeanor.

"It's true, Caleb. It's true."

"This is terrible. An outrage!"

"Why do you say that?" Ingersoll asked. He leaned over closer and peered into Caleb's face.

Caleb felt his heart race. He was suddenly frightened. He could have bitten off his own tongue in that moment. For the truth was before him, deep and immutable in the stony face of Nathaniel Ingersoll. Was this not proof enough of the pattern he had wondered about two nights before?

How could he have forgotten? Ingersoll himself was the uncle of Captain Jonathan Walcott, Mary Walcott's father. And Walcott was a brother-in-law to Thomas Putnam!

Such was the dark design. And the dark design burned ever stronger. As Caleb looked over at the bar, Captain Walcott and his brother-in-law, Thomas Putnam, sat with their elbows resting on the wood counter as they sipped their cider. They looked quite satisfied, as if they had already eaten their noonday meal. And yet here was Sarah Ingersoll, the daughter of Nathaniel, just setting down two immense plates before them, laden with large joints of meat and several potatoes.

"I mean," Caleb muttered to Nathaniel Ingersoll, "that the awful affliction of the girls is a terrible thing."

He quickly walked off. He would not take cider in this tavern. It was clear that Nathaniel Ingersoll's business had changed. Where once he had been a close friend of Virginia and Jacob Chase, now he was part of the pattern, the design, the conspiracy. Was there no one in this village to whom one could talk sense?

He was tempted to turn around and leave the village, for the whole place suddenly seemed to be tainted. He had looked in vain for the likes of John Procter or Daniel Andrews. But none of these sensible men were about. Yet, if he left, what would be accomplished? And if he stayed, he might learn something. He felt he must keep himself abreast. If things got too bad. . . .

He did not finish the thought, but instead joined the others and walked toward the meeting.

*   *   *

With the latest witch safely in manacles, the afflicted girls now sat quietly in the first row of the meetinghouse. They appeared somewhat wan from their morning exertions. But it reminded Caleb of a calm before a storm, or the eerie quiet he heard sailors talk about that was at the very eye of a hurricane.

Some strange madness seeped through the air like the peculiar sulfurous odors that came with the rage of a storm. The calm did not deceive; the piety of the congregation did not discourage the rage in their breasts; their placid faces did not camouflage the fear behind everyone's eyes. The storm was there and waiting, and baiting those winds of terror and destruction was the thunderous sermon bellowed out by the Reverend Lawson.

"You are therefore to be deeply humbled and sit down in the dust, considering the . . . hand of God in singling out this place, this poor village, for the first seat of Satan's tyranny and to make it . . . the rendezvous of devils. . . . I am thus commanded to call and cry . . . to you. Arm! Arm! Arm! Let us admit no parley, give no quarter. Prayer is the most proper and potent antidote against the serpent's venomous operations. . . . Pray! Pray! Pray!"

The minister's face became contorted from his exhortations. And in their hearts, many listeners believed that the Old Serpent himself was just behind the door of the meetinghouse. Any moment he was ready to slither into the congregation and coil in the bosom — in the very heart — of the next witch.

Caleb left the meetinghouse, intent on getting back to Salem Town and away from the village as fast as he could. He must begin to think, and think hard.

He had to have a plan. It was only a matter of time before . . . Once more he cut off the thought. Just then, an arm reached out and grabbed his own. He felt fingers dig into the homespun of his sleeve.

"Caleb!"

"Goody Dawson."

"Where were you when your mother needed you on shearing day, now that Gilly's up and left her? I daresay she had a time with our rams, but then again she has uncommon strength for a woman." The small, dark eyes gleamed bright and hard in the soft puffiness of the old lady's face. "She nicked them good, she did. Next time, you come and help her. But as I was saying, your mother has uncommon strength for a woman!"

Caleb could scarcely speak. He did not remember what he said to get away. But as soon as he did get away, he headed for the Frost Fish Brook pier to catch a ride downstream with Daniel Andrews.

CHAPTER
TWENTY-TWO

Mary Warren watched as Elizabeth Procter bent over the pot she was stirring. It hung from the wrought-iron arm in the hearth.

Elizabeth pressed a handkerchief to her nose and mouth, for the fumes of the mutton stew were noxious to her at this early stage of her pregnancy. But Mary Warren did not feel sympathy; she only felt disgust. The woman complained all the time, whether she was pregnant or not. At least that was what Mary thought. And her husband did more than his share for her.

Yet Mary noticed that Elizabeth Procter's husband had become more distant from his wife in recent days. She was sure it was so. And why not? The woman did not lift a finger to help him. Never fetched his pipe. Didn't even pour him a mug of cider when he came in from mucking out the barn, and this was after a long day at his tavern.

Procter's Inn and Tavern was ever so much busier than Ingersoll's because it was on a more traveled road. The poor man came home exhausted by the day's end, and then he usually went back after supper for several more hours. Did his wife care? No, not a bit, thought Mary.

With good reason John Procter was growing colder toward his wife. And the very thought warmed Mary Warren. Now she heard his heavy stomp coming through the mud room. Mary straightened her cap.

As soon as John Procter entered a room, space and objects seemed to contract and shrink. He was a giant of a man, standing closer to seven feet than six. His huge, broad frame scraped the ceiling beams. He looked younger than his sixty years despite the streaks of gray in his beard. Mary ran to the pipe box and got out his favorite pipe.

"Here, Master," she said. Her voice was light and breathless.

"Thank you, Mary." He inclined his head slightly and looked directly into her eyes. It felt as if a million butterflies were beating in her chest. It wasn't just her imagination. He was noticing her now in a new way.

Then he turned his back and spoke in a gruff voice. "You been behaving yourself?"

Whom was he speaking to?

"Mary!" he demanded more sharply. "You been behaving? You haven't been sneaking down to them examinations or any of that foolishness in the village?"

Mary's heart sank. They treated her like a child, and here she was almost twenty. She had not had any more fits. She had not gone near the afflicted girls. He had beaten her for doing it. The color rose in her cheeks.

"I told you I wouldn't. I am almost twenty. Don't you trust me?"

John Procter turned around slowly. His massive shoulders blocked the light from the kerosene lamp, but she could still see his features. They were dark and menacing. "I trust you to stick to your spinning."

He didn't trust her. Not at all. It was clear. But Mary threw him back a look, bold and hot; he might not trust her, but she knew he thought her to be no child.

"It's not that we don't trust you, dear," Elizabeth Procter whined. "It's only that the times are most strange." She paused. "And dangerous."

Mary Warren tossed her head in a saucy, defiant gesture, and she stomped out of the room.

From the shadows in a corner, Sarah Procter observed the exchange. She was rocking the youngest of the Procter babies in her arms. How she hated Mary Warren! How could her mother tolerate the way Mary looked at her father? Did she not see the boldness in the girl's eye? Why was her mother always so gentle and forgiving with her?

Ever since Mary had come to their family, she had been nothing but trouble. She was lazy, and she was only nice to the children when their parents were around. The rest of the time she had them do not only their own chores, but hers as well.

Then, when she had started sneaking off to Tituba's kitchen, it had become even worse. That was when she had started casting those bold looks toward Sarah's father, and waiting on him hand and foot. 'Oh, here's your pipe, Master. Oh, I'll help you with the milking. I know you had a long day at the tavern. Such a hard life you lead, Master.' She had even tried to accompany him to the tavern one afternoon to help in the kitchen.

Oh, how Sarah and the other children had loved it when her father beat Mary for having the fits and then set her to spinning.

But it was for the fits that he had beaten her, not for anything else. Sarah wasn't sure if her father quite realized the rest. But it was her mother's ignorance that worried Sarah more than her father's. It was not just that Mary Warren fussed over their father and was almost rude to their mother. It was more. Sometimes she caught Mary looking at her mother in a very scary way — cold and calculating, as if she knew something about Elizabeth Procter that no one else did. It chilled Sarah to the bone.

Long past midnight, as the moon climbed in the sky, the house of John Procter was still. But four people did not sleep. Elizabeth Procter lay awake, worrying about the child she carried in her womb.

She had borne five children already. This was to be her sixth. She was an experienced midwife, the best in the region, and often women preferred her ways to those of Dr. Griggs. But she was worried about this pregnancy.

It didn't feel right. She might lose it, and perhaps that would be a blessing in these strange times. Imagine a world in which a child like little Dorcas Good was sent to prison. It was on the very day that she had heard the news about little Dorcas that she had begun to get sicker in this pregnancy. Now she imagined this baby, curled up in her womb, willing itself not to grow. Why would it ever want to be born?

John Procter lay beside her. He feigned sleep, but his wife knew he was not asleep. Yet they were both too tired to talk. He wondered if his wife had heard about his outburst at Ingersoll's Ordinary when he had been outraged after they had hauled Rebecca Nurse off to prison. He had completely lost his head.

"Hang them all!" he had shouted. "Hang every one of the crazed wenches." He never should have said it in public. But he was a man of strong temper and just nature. He had seen the thin smile on Nathaniel Ingersoll's face as he had shouted his curse on the girls.

He had been a fool. Was he not playing right into Ingersoll's hands with such an outburst? How

Nathaniel would love to have the only tavern in the countryside. Bridget Bishop's was no real competition for him, but Procter's was.

John Procter sighed and rolled over on his side. Here he was, nigh onto sixty-one, and still he could not temper his ways.

Mary Warren lay on her pallet in an attic room. Her bed was directly over the Procter's. Sometimes, in the middle of the night, she could hear its rhythmic creaks. She was no girl. She knew what went on. He was a robust man, John Procter, but she'd caught him looking at her often.

She remembered the first time. It had been a hot summer day in the barn when she was helping with the hay bales and had loosened her bodice and untied the strings of her blouse neck. She saw how he looked at her when she bent over for the bales. He bent, too, at precisely the same time, in the same rhythm.

She had not heard the squeaking of his bed for many months now. It made her happy and warm. She would bide her time. And it was merely a matter of time, she felt. She wouldn't have to do a thing.

Sarah Procter shared a bed with her two younger sisters. The little ones slept now, hot and damp against her. But she could not sleep. Her heart had turned grim with her hatred for Mary Warren. She knew the afflicted girls were full of nonsense; for indeed, if her own terrible, waking dreams had any power at all, they would have left marks on Mary Warren. There was never anybody more ripe for the Devil than Sarah Procter. Had she a shape, she would send it out not merely to pinch and bite, but to squeeze the living breath from the milky-white throat of Mary Warren.

Sarah Procter dreamed of murder.

CHAPTER
TWENTY-THREE

Mary Chase talked softly to the young mare as she guided her along the road. They had bought the horse when it was just a colt, a few months before her father had died. Jacob Chase had set himself to training it for Mary, but he was dead before the horse was saddle broken.

Caleb and Mary had finished the job. The mare had been a skittish thing, and it was not wise to take her out when the roads were slick with mud. But now, this first week in April, a light, dry, south-westerly breeze blew, and it had not rained for more than two weeks. The buds on the trees were swelling. The grass was losing its pale winter color, and soon there would be dandelions and buttercups springing up like yellow stars across the meadows.

It would have been a perfect day to be out riding except for one thing. Today was the day that Mary learned of Elizabeth Procter's arrest for witchcraft.

When Mary's mother had heard the news, she had sunk down into her chair and wept. She had ordered Mary out of the house. Insisted that she go for a ride on the mare. But Mary could not enjoy the ride. She did not look for the secret life of the fields, the quivering vole, the kestrel soaring above. Nor did she listen for the spring peepers or the mad gurgle of the streams unlocked from their wintry grip. She felt numb. Her commands to the horse were automatic and unthinking.

Usually she delighted in the feeling of the quick muscle and energy. She looked forward to a good gallop when the road was clear and hard. But today, she felt listless and detached.

Ahead on the road she saw the figures of three other riders. Almost immediately she could tell that one of the riders was Ann Putnam junior. Ann was an accomplished rider and had a distinctive way of sitting on her horse. They would be passing one another soon. There was no avoiding the group, for this was the road leading to Topsfield, and Mary had already passed the last turnoff, just a quarter mile back. There would be no getting off the road now.

On either side, flanking Ann Putnam, were Mary Walcott and Mercy Lewis. Mary thought that perhaps she could pass them with the briefest of greetings. But it was not to be. The girls seemed eager to talk, and they halted their horses.

"How do you do, Mary?" asked Ann Putnam. She lifted her chin in the air and fixed Mary with a steady gaze.

"Fine, fine."

"And your brother?" Mercy Lewis giggled.

"He is fine."

"Still working, is he, in the Storey Yard in Salem Town?"

"Yes, yes."

"And where are you going on this fine day?"

"Oh, just out for a ride. The mare needs her exercise. She gets impish if she is not exercised properly."

"Yes, I can see that," said Ann Putnam, rather haughtily. "We are on our way to Topsfield."

"Oh," Mary said.

"Yes," Mercy Lewis told her. "We've been called there."

"Called there?"

The girls exchanged glances and then gave Mary a withering look.

"You have not heard?" Ann Putnam said with studied coolness.

"Heard what?"

"John Dahl, the richest farmer in Topsfield, and the Reverend Benton and the justice of the peace have sent for us. Some families there are most horribly afflicted, and we have been called upon to root about for the source of the witchcraft."

"They are going to conduct a scientific experiment," said Mary Walcott. "And they cannot do it without us."

"Oh," Mary said, unable to say more.

154

"So we best be off," Ann said gaily. "The whole town awaits us."

They bade each other good-bye, and the girls trotted off.

Mary Chase turned in her saddle to watch them, the simple village girls whose fame had spread as far as Topsfield now. Soon they would be exchanging their homespun dresses for embroidered magisterial robes. Wouldn't they love that! And perhaps caps dripping with frothy lace swags.

Suddenly Mary had an urge to watch the girls participating in this scientific experiment. If she waited ten minutes, not more, they would be out of sight, and she could take the turn off the road a quarter mile back. She knew a shortcut from that road that could get her to Topsfield faster.

Mary tethered her horse in a thicket of trees and crept toward a hedge of laurel bushes that was behind the local inn. From here she had a good view of the town green, and she could see a number of distinguished-looking gentlemen in addition to a throng of villagers who had gathered. No doubt they intended to meet the girls here when they arrived.

Twenty minutes later, with Ann Putnam in the lead, the girls rode into town. People hung back as the reverend and another gentleman greeted them. Both men addressed the girls with a formality and dignity reserved for the most august visitors and never shown to mere children. And then they led them to a house opposite the inn.

As soon as the girls, the dignitaries, and several other people entered the house, Mary came out from behind the hedge. A group of at least twenty people remained milling about outside the house, and Mary knew, in towns like these, any stranger was immediately recognized. So she avoided the people and circled back behind the house.

This was much better. She could see into the room where the sick person lay, for it was at the rear of the house. She dared not peek in the window, but the window was open, and even standing twenty feet away in a thicket of alders, she could hear what transpired inside the house.

"Yes! Yes!" came the cry. Mary thought it was Ann Putnam's voice, but she could not be sure. "I see it just there — above Goody Fallow's head. She is perched most fearsome. She is drooling bile onto her chest."

"Yes, I see it! I see it! It's green and terrible. She pinches Goody Fallow. See her arm flinch!"

There was now an outburst and much commotion. Piercing shrieks erupted.

Then all was quiet. From her hiding place in the alders, Mary began to see people moving down the road. The three girls soon appeared. They walked at a stately pace. Three dignified men walked in front of them, two behind.

A thin stretch of woods paralleled the road, and

Mary could move through it, silent and camouflaged. She could still see what was happening. She watched.

The number of villagers had grown. At least fifty people were now in attendance. But the crowd was quiet to a point of reverence as the girls passed by, stepping aside to make an avenue for them.

In Salem Village, the girls were treated with wonder and amazement, but people still, for the most part, tended to remember that they were just girls — and many skeptics never let them forget this. Here in Topsfield, however, it was a different story. Mary followed them from house to house for well over an hour. It was always the same. A family member would come out and welcome them with trembling respect, then lead them into the sickroom. It reminded Mary of the stories in the Bible of the cripples who had awaited the healing touch of Jesus and his disciples.

At each house, the girls reported variations of the same — the green, horrid bile dripping on the victim, a witch at the head or hovering over the chest. As soon as their pronouncements began, other people, particularly younger members of a household, would break into scalding shrieks and fall down on the floor. Their visions came at a fast and furious pace and seemed to have a powerful contagion. Almost before the girls entered a house, people in the crowd would begin a howl and see desperate apparitions flying above the rooftops.

And yet, Mary wondered, even if the girls could see these specters, how could they name them? The town of Topsfield was a strange one for the three girls. They did not know the people, and they did not know the gossip. Who, for example, was the Sarah Good of this town? Who, with mumbling and outlandish behavior, threatened the smugness of the village folk? Or who had a prosperity and piety to match Rebecca Nurse's? Or who, like Elizabeth Procter, had a husband too bold in his speech? How would the girls know? Perhaps this was what the scientific experiment would reveal. And now, at last, the girls were making their way toward the meetinghouse, where the experiment would be conducted.

The room was so packed that Mary was able to squeeze into the rear without anyone noticing. Ann Putnam, Mary Walcott, and Mercy Lewis stood in front of the room. They had entered a deep trance. Their eyes stared blankly ahead; their limbs appeared rigid, and every now and then their necks or heads would twitch. Mary Walcott drooled a line of spittle down the front of her bodice.

To one side, Mary noticed a cluster of men and women who were blindfolded. The justice of the peace and the Reverend Benton called the first person up. A frail, elderly woman. The test was to be that of touch.

The blindfolded woman's hand was extended

and guided to the hands of the girls. The old lady bent her elbow and clutched it to her bosom. But she was no match for the Reverend Benton and his deacon, who was a strapping man. The deacon pried open her elbow and yanked her forearm so hard, Mary was sure it would spring from its socket. The gnarled hand was guided to Ann Putnam's rigid fingertips.

Almost immediately, Ann's hand became limp. She took a deep breath, blinked, and the blind stare left her eyes. A delightful smile of relief crossed the girl's face. By touching the girl, the poison of the devils that tormented her was forced to flow back into the witch herself, or so it was believed. And this was considered the absolute proof that the old lady was indeed a witch.

Time after time it was proven so, as they led up other men and women from the village.

"But, wait. I don't understand." The whispered voice was hot and desperate. It came from someone standing to the right of Mary. "Goodman Bolt was included because he was above all suspicion. It was part of the experiment to have some in there who couldn't be witches."

"It was the same with Goody Gould."

There was some mumbling amongst the people around Mary that there had only been six or fewer suspected witches. However, by the end of the experiment, the justice of the peace had signed warrants for the arrests of forty witches.

159

Mary left the meetinghouse before the last warrant had been signed.

She had taken the same shortcut back toward home. On this route, she passed Howard's Mill and remembered they were still owed one bag of cornmeal that Goodman Howard had said they could pick up any time. She would stop in now.

As she turned in through the gate to the mill, Mary caught her breath; there was Gilly, and next to him, her head bent forward and bobbing vigorously in conversation, was Goody Dawson. Her husband, Benjamin Dawson, was over by the mill, speaking with Miller Howard. But it appeared to Mary that Goody Dawson and Gilly were in a very intense conversation.

Why should this scene disturb her so? It was not the first time Mary had seen Gilly since Caleb had shouted him off their property. She had skillfully avoided looking at him and had once crossed the road in the village to miss him. But they had seen him in meeting on several occasions since that night. Now, however, it upset her to see him and Goody Dawson together, speaking so animatedly. The two were completely oblivious to her presence. Should she turn around and leave?

No, she had come for her bag of cornmeal, and, by the stars, she would get it!

*　*　*

She rode the mare right up to the hitching post and dismounted. They still had not seen her. She began walking toward the millstone.

Then she felt it, right between her shoulder blades — their stare. The eyes bored into her. But this was not the feeling that stilled her heart; what upset her more was the lingering image of the two heads bent close in conversation. There was a gleam in their eyes that even Mary could see from the distance at which she had been standing.

She had seen that posture before, just three days earlier. She had been in Ingersoll's Ordinary, and Nathaniel Ingersoll and Jonathan Walcott had been bending their heads at nearly identical angles as they whispered, their eyes similarly aglow. Two days later the complaint was filed and signed by them, charging Elizabeth Procter with witchcraft.

It was becoming a familiar posture. The heads of two or three people huddled together and nearly touching, the muffled, throaty voices, the shining eyes. This, Mary realized, was the posture of conspiracy.

Caleb was right. It was only a matter of time.

CHAPTER TWENTY-FOUR

Nothing was turning out the way Mary Warren had imagined, nothing at all. In fact, it was utterly horrid. Even before they had arrested John Procter, when they had just taken his wife, it was not at all the way it was supposed to be. It was not the way she had imagined it, with just herself and the master in the house.

John Procter had sat around all day long, either crying or staring like a dead man into the fire. It had made Mary Warren sick to watch him, sick with disgust, not grief. This big, strapping man shaking like a monster baby with sobs. And he didn't even beat her! If he had at least beaten her, then she could have cried, and perhaps that would have brought him to his senses. He would have then felt sorry for her and appreciated all the hard work she had been doing since Elizabeth had been taken off to prison.

But he didn't care, not one whit. He cared about nothing, not even whether the children were fed and cleaned, or the same for himself, for that matter. There was nothing but work.

She felt like a fool for dreaming of what life would be like when just she and the master were in the house. Of course there were the children, but no bother. Had he been in his right mind, he would have seen how much prettier and younger and livelier she was than that lardy-faced wife of his.

Well, it had only been a week, and then they had come after the master himself. He looked almost pleased to be going.

"I'll see your mother in jail," he had said to the children, but he said nothing to Mary, and he had told Sarah to look after things.

Sarah could have the whole lot, Mary Warren thought, or what was left of it. The sheriff had departed minutes earlier after seizing everything, including the milk cows, half a cord of wood, a plow, a barrel of beer and one of cider. He even took away their cooking pot.

Mary Warren, standing on the Ipswich Road, saw him leave with the wagon piled high and the livestock tethered and trailing behind. The pot and a kettle clanked noisily off the rear quarter, setting up a din as he drove away.

Tears streamed down her face. What was she to do now? The cold reality of her situation and the absolute stupidity of all her fantasies engulfed her. She had been crying so hard that she had not heard anyone approach. But suddenly a dim voice broke through her sobs.

"Why are you crying, Mary Warren?"

She rubbed her face with her apron and blinked. Was that Caleb Chase before her? She could scarcely believe it. He had grown a foot in the past two months, and his face spots were gone, and his shoulders had broadened. Oh, how could he see her this way! She sniffled, and with a futile gesture, began dabbing her eyes and patting her face.

"I was just coming back from a visit to my family and was heading back to the town when I heard your crying."

"Oh, Caleb!" she wailed and then flung herself against his chest. He smelled salt-fresh and piney. And although he wasn't as tall as John Procter, she could feel his blood pumping and his energy. It excited her.

"What is it, Mary? What is it?"

"Even the pot!" she sobbed. "The pot! The pot!"

Caleb could not understand what the girl was sobbing about — a pot? But she kept pressing her body into his, and muttering about a pot.

"What are you talking about?" Caleb took a step back from her and gently pushed her away. "Tell me, what is it, Mary?"

"The sheriff." She sobbed and then gulped.

"Yes, I passed him on the road." And then it dawned on him. "Don't tell me — were those John Procter's cows? And his horses, and that load of furnishings also?"

Mary nodded and stared coldly down the road. "They were, and he even took the kettle and the . . . the . . . the pot!" She burst into sobs once more and threw herself upon Caleb.

He had heard about John and Elizabeth Procter, and he knew that the property of accused witches could be seized, but he thought that it could not be taken away until after a trial. If what Mary was saying was true, how was the poor girl to look after the children? He would have to go to his mother and gather a few things together to bring back.

Mary had collected herself a bit more, and Caleb walked her over to the front stoop of the Procter's house. She was muttering something, but he couldn't understand exactly what it was.

"And to think it began all for sport."

"What? What do you say?"

"It was just a game."

"What was just a game?"

The color began to drain from Caleb's face. A grayness crept across his cheekbones.

"In the beginning, you know, in Tituba's kitchen."

"You mean the little sorceries?"

"Well, yes . . . ." she answered slowly. She thought back to the drizzling November day when Tituba had first stirred the egg yolk into a bowl of water and had seen the figure. Tituba had told Mary that it was a broad giant of a man who was drawn to her. What else was Mary to think? She had already felt the heat of John Procter's gaze upon her; so what she had suspected, Tituba had merely said might truly be so. "Yes . . . the little sorceries were just a game, and the rest, you know, for sport."

"What rest?"

Mary looked at the scuffed toes of her boots. "The girls, you know, the fits . . . they did but dissemble."

"They what?" Caleb roared and jumped to his feet. "They lied, you are saying?"

"Well, a bit, you know."

Mary looked up. She had never in her life seen such a rage.

Caleb yanked her to her feet. "You mean to tell me all this time they have been lying, and you lied, too, and you knew they were lying, and now your good master and his wife and Rebecca Nurse and Martha Cory and God knows who else have been and will be . . ." Caleb gulped for a breath. His face turned darker. "Oh, you are a loathsome creature!" he said between clenched teeth. And then he spat on her, square in the face.

Caleb was determined that Israel Porter should know of the girls' deceit by the time the sun set.

The madness must be stopped before it was too late.

CHAPTER

TWENTY-FIVE

Mary Chase and her mother had just finished their evening Bible reading and were about to turn down the lamps, snuff the candles, and climb the stairs to bed. Both were exhausted from the day's activities. Lambing season had begun in earnest.

Two lambs had been born before dawn. No sooner had Virginia and Mary gone in to wash off the blood from those births and make a mug of tea, than one of the heifers began birthing. It was a terrible birth, and fortunately Caleb had arrived and helped pull the poor calf out — dead. They were lucky not to lose the mother. So their day had gone. Now, bone weary, they were ready for sleep.

And that was when they heard the hooves on the dirt.

Mary was never quite sure what it was that had made her breath catch before they had even rapped on the heavy wood door. Was it the creak of the cart's wheels? Had she actually heard a clanking of irons? But as soon as she opened the door and the men crowded through, she knew in that instant that nothing would ever be the same again. Her small, warm world began to evaporate into thin air.

"Virginia Chase!" Constable Braybrook bellowed. "In the name of the High Sheriff of the County of Essex, whereas one Thomas Putnam and Benjamin Dawson have filed a complaint against you, having witnessed your shape heeding not the laws of gravity but those of the invisible world while pursuing their families and livestock, afflicting them with great pain and soreness, you are now being charged with practices of witchcraft against these pious families and their kin. You are therefore arrested, and in accordance with the law and in the names of William and Mary of England, it is both willed and commanded that you be imprisoned to await trial for this most horrendous crime of maledict witchcraft."

Mary stood, frozen. A leaden coldness crept through her body.

Except for the pulse throbbing just beneath her jaw, Virginia Chase was very still. Her long, pale face with its delicate contours was luminous.

She could be an angel, Mary thought, alighted from above. This room, the people, the world — all suddenly seemed too coarse for her mother's presence. And as rage began to swell in Mary's heart, her mother seemed to grow more peaceful, more beautiful with each passing second.

She heard a strangled voice. It struck her as odd, for it was her own, but it sounded so different. "How? How can they do this? It's not Benjamin. It's Goody Dawson, is it not, who put him up to this? And Thomas Putnam?"

"Hush!" Virginia said, turning to her. Then she faced the constable and Sheriff Corwin, who stood beside him and Second Constable Willard.

"It is a sickness not of witches that seizes these poor people's souls," Virginia said, addressing them calmly. "It is that of greed. Mark well, Constable Willard: Your wife's family — are they not the second largest landholders, after the Putnams, west of the Village of Salem? And did not one of them marry Rebecca Nurse's daughter? Be careful. And that scrap of land you are interested in — it's owned by the Porters, but disputed by the Putnams. It is only a matter of time before you yourself might be declared a wizard or your wife a witch."

And then Virginia Chase did what no other witch had done. She walked straight up to the three men and looked them all directly in the face with her beautiful, luminous gray eyes. "I forgive you, each and every one of you. For you have become the Devil's instrument, and the Devil is not from the invisible world but from the visible — the world of money and land and failed businesses and disastrous enterprise, and yes . . . yes, of wombs so barren, they have become cauldrons of bitterness."

"Mother!" Mary screamed as Virginia Chase turned and walked out the door with her captors.

CHAPTER
TWENTY-SIX

S he was swimming, swimming into the shallower waters of sleep. She did not want to break through the surface, but rather to sink back into the cool darkness. She fought it hard. If she did not wake up, everything would be all right. There was something she did not want to remember, but she was supposed to remember it. Someone was shaking her now.

"Mary! Mary, wake up."

It was Caleb. What was he doing here? Where was she? There was a lovely smell of wood shavings.

"Mary. Mary! Mary!"

Her eyes opened slowly. Her brother's face, taut, was over her. Then it all came back. Her wild ride on the mare, arriving at the shipyard past midnight, pounding on the shed door. Blurting out the terrible news.

She moaned now, as it washed over her afresh. Her mother was in prison, not more than a quarter mile from this shed. Her mother was in irons.

That had been Mary's last sight of her mother. They had put the chains on her feet and hands just outside the door, by the little herb garden that Virginia had tended so carefully and where she had planted the small shrubs and plants in such pleasing designs. Mary had heard the noise of the iron clasps and the chain links just there by the rosemary.

She closed her eyes. The sound of those manacles near the pleasant garden was an offense, a violence that shook Mary to her bones.

"I'd sooner smear pig droppings on the Bible," she muttered.

"What?" whispered Caleb.

Mary began to cry softly again as she thought of the heavy iron bands being locked around her mother's wrists.

"Mary, there is no time for tears. We must be brave. We must, if we are to save Mother."

"How? How? There is talk of the trials beginning within the next two weeks, or certainly by the first of June, at the latest. There is no way we can save her."

"Don't talk that way, Mary!"

Mary sat up on the pallet now and looked fiercely at her brother. "You do not know, Caleb. You live here in Salem Town, far away from it all. They say the only way to save oneself is to confess — and Mother will never do that. And even if she would, it helps not. Sarah Good confessed, as did Tituba. They are still in prison, and now even little Dorcas is there with her mother!"

"We shall save her, Mary. We must be clever. We shall be clever!" Caleb spoke fiercely. "We must go this morning to the jail and find out when she is to be examined. Then we must go to Israel Porter; and if we need to, we shall go to the new governor himself."

"William Phips? He is not even here yet."

"His ship, the *Nonesuch*, is due in Boston by mid-May. I shall go to him," Caleb said resolutely.

"You will?"

"Yes."

And Caleb knew he would go, but he did not want to raise Mary's spirits too high. He had heard that although Phips was a decent man, he was one of high adventure, often more interested in challenges abroad than at home. He had captained ships around the world, found sunken Spanish treasure in the Bahamas. And it was said that his hot-blooded temperament drew him toward a fight with the French and the Indians. It was his goal to subdue Canada. So a New England widow accused of witchcraft might be thin gruel for a man more buccaneer than governor. Such squabbles might not befit his heroic nature and his fiery dreams of glory.

The magistrates wasted no time. Virginia's preliminary examination was set for that very afternoon.

"What do you mean? We cannot be at our mother's examination?"

"There will be only women at this first examination. They must unclothe Goody Chase and go over her body for witchmarks!"

Caleb and Mary both gasped.

"Witchmarks!" Caleb whispered.

The sheriff looked down his long nose; it perched like a slender bird between his fleshy cheeks. His disdain was evident.

"A mark of the Devil is evidence and proof of guilt. Any teat or unnatural protuberance or mark is known as the means by which a wizard or witch can suckle familiars. The Reverend Cotton Mather himself wrote on this point. We have found suckling excrescences and extra nipples on many so far. Even little Dorcas Good had a nubbin on her small finger through which she suckled her snake."

Caleb and Mary could not speak. The horror surrounding them seemed to thicken by the minute.

Finally, Mary managed to regain her tongue. "And will this examination be conducted here at the prison in Salem Town?"

"Yes, there is a special room off the magistrates', just down there." He pointed at a corridor behind him. "Such examinations are conducted there. The women will be arriving momentarily. You best be on your way now, children. There should be some news by this evening."

They had no sooner left when Mary turned on her heels.

"Where are you going?" Caleb asked.

"I mean to get into that room, Caleb. I'll find a way."

"How?"

She pulled the hood of her cloak further forward on her head. "Can you see my face?"

"Not too well."

"Good. There's a niche just outside the room of the sheriff's, where we were. It's not large, just my size, really. I shall rest there till the women come, and then I'll go into the room with them. I shan't be recognized."

"Mary, be careful."

"I shall be. And I shall be brave, too, Caleb, just as you told me."

It was easier than Mary had thought. And she was briefly emboldened by this venture. For she felt that if she could somehow work around these forces, right here within the prison, there might be hope for helping her mother.

She and Caleb had to be continuously vigilant. All of their efforts must go into saving their mother. They had made the decision that morning not to worry about the farm. Sheriff Corwin or the constables would no doubt be there in a matter of days to confiscate everything. And property was nothing compared to this.

Next to the door through which she had come, she found a vast cupboard in which the magistrates' robes hung. The door was slightly ajar, and no one noticed when Mary slipped into its shadowy interior. Here she now stood amongst the hanging robes. Ann Putnam senior stood not two feet in front of her, speaking merrily with Mercy Lewis and Elizabeth Hubbard.

"They shall be leading her in any moment, Sheriff Corwin told me." Ann Putnam smoothed her hands over her cap and straightened her shoulders in anticipation. Had Mary a knife, she could have plunged it into that narrow, straight back without a second thought. But no, she would have had a second thought. For that was precisely the point: She and Caleb must not let their passions get the best of them. They must proceed with utmost caution.

Suddenly Mary's knees grew weak. She pressed her fist to her mouth and felt the blood drain from her face. The sheriff and two constables were leading Virginia Chase into the room. What had happened to her dear mother?

The luminous beauty of the night before had been completely extinguished. A gray shell moved woodenly into the room, the eyes not focusing, the mouth hung half open. She wore no cap. Her hair was matted and dirty, and one side of her face appeared scraped or bruised.

Another man came in just before the proceedings were to start. He drew out a notebook and took a seat at a table where he would have a good view. It was the Reverend Deodat Lawson.

"Women, you may proceed," the sheriff intoned. But Mary did not notice him leave the room, nor did she see Magistrate Hathorne, nor Corwin, nor the reverend leave the room, either. So there would be men present.

Mary was confused. She thought no men were to be there. Her mother was to be stripped bare in front of their former minister, who would sit and observe her naked body while writing in his notebook. Mary closed her eyes tightly and swallowed, fighting off waves of nausea.

When she opened them a few seconds later, she saw Goody Dawson and Elizabeth Parris, along with Ann Putnam senior, approach her mother. The Reverend Lawson craned his neck and began writing again in his book.

"Now off with that bodice and blouse, Goody Chase," Goody Dawson said briskly.

But of course her mother could not undo the buttons or strings, for her hands were chained. So she merely stared ahead. Even from where Mary hid, she could see the pulse throbbing just below her mother's jaw.

Goody Dawson stepped up to Virginia and began unlacing the bodice strings. She yanked it down.

Elizabeth Parris seemed to hang back, not having a taste for this stripping, but Ann Putnam tore open the buttons of the chemise, and in one quick, brutal gesture, she pulled down the smock.

Virginia stood naked now, her breasts exposed.

"Ah, ha!" cried Goody Dawson. "What is this! Already the mark by which she suckles her familiar. A third teat, I do say."

Goody Dawson's plump finger jabbed between Virginia's full breasts.

"What? What?" Ann Putnam said excitedly. The other women pressed closer to examine what Goody Dawson had found.

"See, there it is — a red gouge between her breasts. A little hook-shaped mark. So convenient, is it not, Goody Chase, for suckling?"

It was then that Mary remembered the piglets, born two months before, that she and her mother had carried about for days next to their skin. And how Virginia's piglet, when it had become stronger, had scratched her on the chest. However, these women, who were devils incarnate themselves, would swear that the piglet had been Virginia's familiar, and through it, she visited her evil upon the world.

But how had Goody Dawson found that mark so quickly? It was very pale, for even Elizabeth Parris said so. She was having trouble seeing it.

Then another dreadful realization struck Mary. It was Gilly, of course! Gilly — who had perched beneath her mother's window, watching Virginia undress each night. He would have seen the mark when it was fresher. And it was Gilly and Goody Dawson who she, Mary, had seen with their heads bent in talk at the miller's, just a week before. Gilly knew of the mark, and all he had to do was tell Goody Dawson that he had seen Virginia suckling a familiar at it between her breasts.

Through the narrow opening in the wardrobe, Mary watched in anguish as the women lifted her mother's skirts and began their minute examination for other marks of the Devil. Of all the fiends and flames of destruction that the Reverend Parris and Deodat Lawson had ever painted in their sermons, none were as hellish as these women now gathered around Mary's mother. They poked their fingers into her as they looked for the Devil's marks.

There was no God in such a world. Of this, Mary was sure. Satan had won, and he was on his knees, peering under the skirts, examining the thighs of her mother. There was a lewdness in the room that would have put the cities of Sodom and Gomorrah to shame.

Mary waited until everyone had left before she slipped out of the building. Her mother had been removed to her cell where she would wait to be tried as a witch, along with the others awaiting trial in prisons in Boston and Ipswich as well as in Salem.

Soon the jails would be overflowing with accused witches as the afflicted girls and the Putnam family stepped up the pace of accusation. On April 18, Bridget Bishop, along with Giles Cory, Abigail Hobbs, and Mary Warren, were arrested. Mary had not kept quiet about the afflicted girls pretending, and although Caleb was the first to hear her remarks, he was not the last. Shortly after that, the girls began to distance themselves from Mary, and then, very soon, she was cried out upon and hauled off to prison to join her master's wife. On April 21, nine more were accused, including Mary Esty, the sister of Rebecca Nurse.

On April 21, Ann Putnam's father, Thomas Putnam, wrote Magistrates Hathorne and Corwin the following letter: "We thought it our duty to inform your honors of what we conceive you have not heard, which are high and dreadful . . . at which our ears do tingle."

The information that made Thomas Putnam's ears tingle had been provided by his daughter. Ann Putnam junior had seen in a dream the specter of George Burroughs, the former minister of Salem, who had since moved away after a dispute with her father. In her spectral dream, Burroughs's dead wife had appeared to Ann in winding sheets and told how, in fact, he had murdered her, as well as his second wife, with his own hands. They had not died of natural causes, as was thought.

Although Ann Putnam junior was only three years old at the time Burroughs had been minister in Salem Village and could not have possibly remembered what he looked like, she identified his "shape" easily. No one doubted her word. The spectral evidence was accepted in full, without question.

A week later, George Burroughs, former minister to Salem Village, was arrested and taken away from his family in Wells, Maine. So it went. . . .

CHAPTER
TWENTY-SEVEN

Within two days of Virginia's arrest, the sheriff arrived at the Chase farm to clear out the property. He had to have help, for there were ten head of sheep, five cows, the draft horse, and the mare. Two wagons and a hackney were seized as well.

Jacob Chase certainly had prospered. A shame his wife was a witch; who knew, perhaps Jacob had been a wizard, the sheriff thought as he drove the hackney with the mare hitched to it. He had tucked in the English pewter where no one could see it. He often would keep the smaller objects rather than hand them over to the court. He thought of them as a commission of sorts for all the trouble he went to in order to keep the village safe from witches. What was a pewter plate or bowl here and there compared to these heifers and the ewes? They'd fetch a pretty penny.

Mary was to stay in Salem Town at the shipyard. Master Jeremy would allow it and not mention anything to the owners. Caleb felt it was far too dangerous for her to stay in the village.

Mary managed to keep herself out of sight. On this day, however, the day after her mother's examination, she had gone back to the farm, arriving just hours after the sheriff had been there and confiscated everything. As she walked through the strange silence of the empty house, she felt a mixture of sadness and genuine relief. They had worked so hard to achieve what they had. Yet now there would be nothing to focus on except finding a way to free her mother. There were no animals to feed, no fences to mend, no fields to plow, no wool to spin. There was just her mother.

They had, she observed, certainly taken everything — every stick of furniture, and every pot and kettle. She walked upstairs to her old bedroom. It was just after mid-day, and the sun sloped in through the diamond-shaped windowpanes at a steep angle. Every dust mote danced its own slow dance in the angled light.

The room seemed warm and stuffy. She would not linger. Then, on the floor, she spotted the dovetailed box. The sheriff and his men had removed the fine walnut bureau that had been her grandmother's and had come from England years before, but they had left the box that Caleb had made. She picked it up and opened the lid.

The lupine seeds rested inside. She stood for a

moment in the slant of sunlight and looked at the seeds at the bottom of the beautifully crafted box. Something deep inside her began to stir. There was a dim voice, a memory, words of her father, something he had said long, long ago.

Yes, it came to her now. He had called it one of God's miracles, that when forests burned and the land stood charred and not a green thing could be seen, that silently, under the blackness of it all, an invisible green was at work; that pinecones and sheaths of seed pods scorched in the blaze often popped open beneath the warm ashes.

The seeds themselves would lie dormant under the protection of layers of charred debris until finally the warm rains of spring coaxed them forth, and thus a new growth came where once fires had burned. From absolute destruction, life grew, green and burgeoning with the promise of a new forest.

Mary looked down at the dovetailed box in her hand. Why had they taken everything but this? The box must be a sign. A sign of hope. For without hope, life was intolerable and made no sense. Without hope, they might all just as well die. Gradually, Mary felt the stirrings of the God she had ceased to believe in when she had stood in the vast cupboard among the magistrates' robes.

Mary peered into the box once more, then shut it and held it even tighter. "I will believe in God," she whispered to the sunlight. "I will believe in a

Lord of lupine seeds and silent green beneath charred timber and fresh salt breezes; I will believe in a God who makes human hands to do fine joinery work, and steer a ship smartly through a gale. I will believe in a God who makes hope possible and faith not a dream."

CHAPTER
TWENTY-EIGHT

Mary and Caleb sat in the shed of the ship-yard. Mary wrapped, in one more layer of cloth, the last of the butter she had churned before the sheriff had come to confiscate their animals and property.

Caleb carefully folded some scraps of canvas that he had been able to get from the sailmaker. Although stiff, this would make some sort of sheeting for his mother's pallet in prison.

They had been allowed to make weekly visits, one of the few concessions the authorities would allow. Their mother had now been imprisoned for almost three weeks, and this was to be their third visit.

The new governor's ship, the *Nonesuch*, had arrived in Boston harbor two days earlier, and Mary hoped that this would be the last visit they would have to make before their mother was set free. She trusted that Governor Phips, being a practical man, would see the insanity that was spreading across the colony and put an end to it.

With their bundles tidily in order, Mary and Caleb set off for the prison. As they walked, Mary wondered how Mary Warren would be this day. One never knew. Since her arrest, she had alternated between periods of lucidity and complete confusion. She had never had any real fits in prison. But she was treated as a special prisoner.

There was no need to bring clean linens or butter for Mary Warren. She was given these things by the authorities, for they wanted something from her. Every day the magistrates took Mary Warren into a separate room where they tried, for hours on end, to extract a confession from her. Had not John Procter brought the book to her and threatened to put hot tongs down her throat if she did not sign? But Mary would not turn on her master.

Today, as the jailer led Caleb and Mary into the cell where more than half a dozen witches sat in filth, they did not see Mary Warren. And why was their mother not standing where she usually did, by the small, high grate that let in paltry slivers of light?

"They are chained!" Caleb's voice fell like a stone in the dank cell.

"No!" Mary shouted as she spied her mother. Virginia was collapsed in a heap against the granite wall. Her ankles already looked puffy around the black clasps that encircled them. Her arms lay listless, and from her wrists, an ugly metal chain connected her to an iron ring in the floor. Her left eye was infected and nearly swollen shut. But with her good eye, she looked straight at her children.

"It's the new governor's order." She spoke quietly.

"Yes," said the jailer crisply. "The power of these witches is something to be reckoned with. Their familiars still torment the poor girls something fierce. So Governor Phips ordered the making of new chains, suitable for prison use. The ones we use for arrest do not work so well here. We just got our delivery yesterday. You will find the chains charged to your mother's account."

"Mary Warren got out just in time," Virginia said.

"She confessed?" Caleb asked.

"She did indeed," the jailer told them.

"Right here." Virginia smiled thinly. "It was a beautiful thing to watch. She was positively blissful as she told them how she had felt the shape of John Procter hovering above her; then, when she described how he reached for her, she arched her back so prettily toward this vision of a man. It was then she had signed the book he had offered."

"Yes, Goody Chase," the jailer said. "You'd be sensible to do likewise and confess, what with the way your feet are puffing under these cuffs."

"I shall not sell my soul to save my feet." Virginia spat the words out.

* * *

They were only allowed a few minutes. Mary cleaned her mother as best she could and applied some ointment to her eye.

"I heard that Sarah Osburne died in Boston prison," Virginia said. "It's worse there than here. And they transported that poor little child Dorcas Good there to be with her mother. And Lord knows if Rebecca Nurse still lives."

"We went to Israel Porter. He is trying everything. He, of all people, might be able to reach the new governor."

"I hold out no hopes for a man who feels he must put broken women in chains. Your father always said that Phips enjoyed fighting Indians and pirates more than governing men."

"Well, we shall see," said Caleb as he vigorously rubbed his mother's legs to ease the pain and swelling.

"What do you mean, Caleb?" Virginia asked warily.

"We plan to go and see the governor, Mary and I."

"Oh Caleb, dear boy!" She ran her fingers through his thick hair. "Trouble yourself no more for me." And then Virginia took her children's hands. "Children, listen to me. This is the last time you may come to visit me."

"What do you mean, Mother?" Tears sprang to Mary's eyes.

189

"It is no longer safe for you. You must let go of me. It will be the kindest thing you can do."

"Let go?" They both uttered the words as if they were from a strange language.

"Yes, and I shall then be able to let go of you. This is the natural way."

"Natural?" Caleb said, his voice filled with astonishment. "You call this natural?" He looked down at his mother's chained ankles.

"No, not this, of course, not this. But I mean that all parents must learn to let go of their children. You let them go so they may enjoy the full life, the better life of love and building a family and independence and fulfilling work. My parents let me and my sisters and brother go. You cannot keep them as babies forever. If I do not let you go, they will take you. Chases are not made to be taken. Both of you must leave Salem. You must go to Richmond. You will be safe there. Your uncle Farnham is there."

"But what about you, Mother?" Mary asked. Tears were streaming down her face.

"I have had a wonderful life. Tomorrow I turn thirty-seven. I have had thirty-six wonderful years. Seventeen with your dear father. I have known love and hard work. I have borne two children and never lost a one. I have learned to coax sustenance from the earth and to make a home warm and as tight as a ship in a tossing sea. What more can I ask of my God than this?

190

"You must not cry for me. You must rejoice in my thirty-six blessed years, and as your last gift to me, give me the hope that you each may have the chance to enjoy perhaps thirty-six more years yourselves, in addition to your twelve and fifteen so far. Give me this gift."

She held each child's hand to her cheeks. They felt her roughened skin. "You must do this." The whispered words were hot in their palms.

"I would not even know how to get to Richmond," Mary said in a small voice as they left the prison.

"It doesn't matter," Caleb said fiercely.

"What do you mean? You mean we aren't going?"

"Of course not."

But from the look in Caleb's eyes, she knew that he had some destination in mind. "Where are we going?"

"As I said, to Boston. To see Governor Phips."

CHAPTER
TWENTY-NINE

"Spectral evidence! Sounds like a fart in the breeze to me. Listen, Stoughton, you know what you can do with the damn hags and whores — yes, yes, shove 'em up your . . . oh, don't go all limp on me. But what in tarnation are people carrying on about? A bleeding 'invisible world'? We got a very visible enemy up in Canada. I came here to fight Indians and French, not witches. You take care of this witch thing. . . . What? Of course I believe in the Devil. Good God, man, I've been a sailor on the Spanish main. I've seen the Devil all right!"

The roar of the man's laughter from behind the heavy doors seemed to shake the very foundations of the building.

Mary and Caleb sat quietly where they had been told to wait in an anteroom of the office of Governor William Phips. They had been hearing the railings of the new governor for the past quarter of an hour. It was impossible not to hear it, much to the profound embarrassment of the clerk who sat behind a high desk on a platform and tried to look unruffled.

Caleb had not heard such salty language since he had spent a week on the frigate *Scorpion* replacing quarterdeck planks when the ship had come into Salem harbor. The clerk was looking absolutely green now as more curses exploded behind the closed doors. The harder he tried to pretend he was not hearing the foul language, the greener he became. Soon the clerk was trembling.

"Jesus, Mother, and Mary!" the voice roared from behind the door. "They call this friggin' spring in Boston? Hah! It's colder than a witch's teat in January!"

Suddenly there was a small crash. Something splashed across the floor. The young clerk rose, stared at the dark lake of ink. He then reached behind the high desk and took his broad-brimmed black hat from a peg. Placing it carefully on his neatly tied hair, he looked directly at the children.

"Tell the governor I have quit." With that, he walked out of the Town House.

Caleb and Mary had left Salem that morning well before dawn. By sun up, they had rounded the Lynn marshes to Noddle's Island. From Noddle's, they took a ferry across the harbor to Boston Town. Neither Caleb nor Mary had ever seen Boston.

As they approached on the ferry, seagulls

wheeled on an early morning breeze blown in from the sea. Three prominences rose against the Boston shore: Copp's Hill in the North End, Fort Hill in the South End, and the steep slopes of Beacon Hill toward the west. Small wooden houses scrambled up these hills, and occasionally a brick-and-stone building stood between them. The wharves were crowded with tall masted ships and sailors; they bustled with the movement of longshoremen unloading and loading cargo. Farmers, too, streamed across the Neck to the south, which connected Boston to the mainland. They brought their animals and produce to sell on the Boston Common and in the streets of the town.

Clouds had soon begun to roll in. By the time Caleb and Mary had reached the governor's offices in the Town House on King Street, a drizzling, cold rain had started to fall.

When they had arrived, the young clerk who sat at the high desk looked down upon them and inquired as to their business.

Caleb and Mary had planned what they would say to gain entrance for a meeting with the governor.

"Ships!" Caleb said quickly. "I come from Salem Town and the Storey Yard. I've been sent here by Mr. Storey himself."

Israel Porter had told Caleb of the governor's love of the sea. Caleb had figured that it was better to first lie about his business than to begin with their plea. How many relatives of accused witches had already been to the governor, pleading for mercy? But now that the clerk had quit, Caleb was not sure how to proceed. For it would have been the clerk who would have told the governor that someone from the shipyard was here to see him.

Suddenly the doors burst open. Phips, a giant of a man, stood glowering. Another man, in a long frock coat, scurried around from behind the governor, looking almost as agitated as the clerk. He dashed out of the anteroom.

"What are we doing? Running a bleeding nursery here?" Phips bellowed. He stared directly at Mary and Caleb. He then wheeled around for an explanation from the clerk.

"Where's Horace?"

"He quit," Caleb said.

"Quit? It's the best goddamn job he ever had. Oh, pardon me!" he said suddenly, realizing that Mary was still there. "What's this? Somebody spill their guts on the floor?" He looked at the pool of ink.

"The clerk spilled his inkwell, sir."

"Hrrumph," growled the governor. "So what do you two want?"

"I'm from the Storey shipyard, and — "

"The Storey Yard! They built my first command. Before it was the Storey Yard, it belonged to Isaiah Metcalf. I worked there myself as a carpenter, then shipped out on the *Falcon*. Come, come in, my boy!" He motioned Caleb in. Mary followed. She did not care whether she had been invited or not.

The governor clearly delighted in talking to a boy who had his sights set upon being a master ship carpenter. For the better part of an hour, Sir William went on and on about his own adventures at sea. Caleb had not been able to get a single word in about his mother and the terrible events of Salem.

Now there was a knock on the heavy doors.

"Who is it?" roared the governor.

There was a muffled noise.

"Speak up, goddamnit!" Then he remembered that he no longer had his clerk to usher in visitors. He got up and strode across the floor. It was the man who had scurried out before, and with him was another tall, sallow-looking gentleman of most forbidding countenance.

"Reverend Mather! Good heavens, man, you look rotten. Have you been fasting again?" boomed Phips.

"And praying. Trying to put an end to these grievous troubles."

"Well, I wish to h — " Phips caught himself. "Well, yes. I do pray also that something'll work. Good heavens, man, I came here fully intending to fight Indians and the French. And what do I have but a passel of witches and wizards hooting about. It's making me look like a damn fool to the crown. Come on in."

The men looked at Mary and Caleb. "Oh, this is my friend from the Storey shipyard." Once again, Phips completely ignored Mary. "Don't mind him. All right, down to business: What are we going to do about this confounded thing out in Salem? It's a great distraction."

Distraction! Mary felt the color rise in her cheeks. Caleb shot her a glance. They must be still and listen. If they could not tell their plight to the governor, they might as well find out all they could. There was definitely no logic in upsetting a man of his temperament.

"The point is that Salem Town is a center of prosperity." The governor was speaking more calmly now. "It is the jewel in the colonial crown, if you will. But right now, the whole place is in chaos. The jails are brimming both in Salem and Boston. If you find another witch, I don't know where you'll put her. But the real problem is that all this is causing me to look poorly," Sir William said with a lowered voice.

"And it's not my fault! I'm here to do a job," he added, "and I cannot do it with this mess going on. After all these years of being charterless, of not having a real system of government, we now are going to be able to go with the new charter. But no one seems to appreciate the full implications of the new charter that King William has given us.

"Yes, we shall now be able to have courts and a legal system, but with it comes an enormous expansion of our borders. In addition to our old colonial boundaries of Nantucket and Martha's Vineyard and Plymouth, we now have Maine, Nova Scotia, and the country in between — as far north as the St. Lawrence. This, gentlemen, constitutes a huge exposed border. These witches might be airborne, but by Jove, my troops aren't! You think it was simple taking Port Royal two years ago. . . ."

The Reverend Cotton Mather and William Stoughton had heard it all before. William Phips was Boston's only knight. As such, he was addressed as Sir William. The title had been conferred five years before when he had raised a vast treasure valued at more than three hundred thousand pounds. King James, the previous monarch, had dubbed him William Knight of the Golden Fleece.

Sir William's accomplishments in King William's war to eliminate the hated French from the New World had never gone unnoticed. Two thousand men had been raised, and thirty-four ships sailed for an attack on Quebec under Phips; and although Phips had proved himself less than efficient in this expedition — for it turned out to be fruitless and costly — his reputation emerged untarnished and intact.

Cotton Mather hated war stories. These exploits were coarse compared to his unending war with the invisible world. He considered Phips crude and an inferior, but he desperately needed the man; indeed his own father, Increase Mather, had hand-picked many of the new councillors and was influential in the choice of Phips. So although Massachusetts was ultimately subject to the Crown, the Crown was still far away. And the men who ran the colony were more closely associated with the Mathers than they were to a king. This, after all, was what counted.

Mather liked Phips because he knew that all Phips really wanted to do was fight the French and the Indians. Not a bad idea, for it would strip out Catholicism along with the French and leave an untainted Puritan state.

So what Phips was embarking upon was no less than a crusade in Mather's eyes — but then again, the same could be said for governing the people closer to Boston. For Massachusetts was a theocracy, a government subject first and foremost to the rules of God. And no one was more suitable for guiding a theocracy than the Reverend Cotton Mather himself. Therefore, it was with utter delight that he heard for himself the words that Phips had spoken to Stoughton just an hour before.

"I'm leaving all this witch business to you. You have to clear it up for me. But, Reverend Mather, I want you to keep a close accounting, and I want written reports sent to London. They take a dim view of what is going on here. Now Stoughton here tells me that by next week, the last Wednesday in May, we shall have a General Court sitting. And when will they be ready to try the first witches, Stoughton?"

"We should have the court of Oyer and Terminer ready to sit by June 2, Sir William."

"Good!" boomed Phips. "And as far as I'm concerned, this spectral evidence isn't worth a pinch of pig . . ."

Stoughton coughed violently. One more barnyard expletive, and the reverend would have an apoplexy. Cotton Mather was not well, and Stoughton was depending on him mightily. If they could only curb Phips! Well, soon he would be gone to the north, fighting Indians and Catholics.

"Oh, and tell me, Stoughton, how are the chains working? Keeping the evil contained?"

"Yes, sir. Word from Salem is that it has helped the afflicted children."

"Speaking of children, what happened to those two who were just here? Hey! Hey! Come back," he called to Mary and Caleb as he saw them exiting through the anteroom.

"He is vile! A horrible man! I don't care if he is the governor. He is the one who put them in chains. Don't you see what is happening, Caleb? All our chances, all our hopes, are being lost, one by one. We had hoped for Israel Porter's help, but he said he could do nothing — not even for Daniel Andrews, his own kin, when he was seized last week. And now the governor! Look at him! He doesn't care a whit about what happens. He just wants to get to his foolish wars with the French and the Indians. Well, let me tell you — it's nonsense. The Salem Village girls — Ann Putnam, Mercy Lewis, and that horrid Mary Warren — the whole lot of them is worse than a swarm of Catholics or a town full of Indians."

"Hush, Mary." Caleb looked about. They were standing on the corner of Tremont Street across from the Common, where Boston folk grazed their cows. People were milling all about them. "Next thing, you'll have us arrested for treason."

"But what are we going to do? The trials are to begin in a little more than two weeks. And there is no defense against this spectral evidence, none whatsoever. Ann Putnam can say she sees a bird, a cat, a snake, and claim it is Goody Esty tormenting her. She'll jerk her neck and roll her eyes, and everyone will believe her."

"And they would believe you, too, wouldn't they, Mary — if you would do it and cry out upon them?"

"What are you saying, Caleb?"

"We cannot discuss it here. It is too late to catch the ferry across the harbor to Noddle's. Master Jeremy gave me the name of a public house in the

North End. It's favored by sailors, and we can talk more freely there. The woman will give us a room for very little."

Mary and Caleb walked down King Street toward the wharves and then turned and followed a series of narrow, winding, dark streets.

Everything smelled just awful in Boston. Slop pails were thrown into the streets, and many of the streets were soupy with sewage. Everyone lived practically atop everyone else. To Mary, it seemed to be more of an anthill than a town. There were inns and hostelries tucked here and there, all, it seemed, with colorful names — Noah's Ark, The Peacock Inn, The Red Lyon, The Two Palaverers, with a sign bearing carved likenesses of two gentlemen in cocked hats. Even the streets and alleys bore odd names — Elbow Alley, Sun and Moon Court. The wharves were lined with all manner of boats and ships: shallops and lighters, hoys and sloops. Anchored off the piers were brigs, barks, and ketches.

The children turned onto Ship Street and soon came upon a low, studded wooden house with leaded casement windows. There was a sign above the door with a leaping dolphin. "This is the place," Caleb announced. "The Dolphin."

Inside, the main room had low ceilings and was stained with smoke. Dark shadows hung everywhere, but a cheery din chased away any gloom. The rum flowed freely, and the people were boisterous. A large woman with a sweaty face and a most immodest dress came charging toward them, carrying at least five flagons of ale in her two hands. She was delivering the drink to a table of rowdies across the room. Her cap was askew, and black tendrils of hair escaped from its edges.

Caleb and Mary found a table in a far corner. They ordered a trencher of cod to share and two mugs of cider.

"So what did you mean by what you said up there on King Street, Caleb?" Mary dropped her voice. "That they would believe me if I were crying out?"

Shadows flickered across Caleb's eyes. "It's getting to that, Mary. Cry out or be cried out upon."

"Caleb!"

"I know, I know. If Mother will not sell her soul by confessing falsely, I would never expect you to cry out. I only tell you this, Mary, because now you must completely hide, disappear. You must not show yourself in Salem Village again."

She knew Caleb was right. It would only be a matter of time before the constables would come for her, but she would sooner slit those accused girls' throats with her own hands than cry out upon an innocent soul.

"You should perhaps stay here in Boston."

"Here?" Mary was stunned. "But Caleb!"

"It would only be temporary." He nodded toward the florid-faced woman serving the drink. "Mrs. Pelham is a niece of Master Jeremy. She would be willing to hire you on, to help out here, you know. And I would be able to come every week to see you."

Mary was speechless. Caleb had planned all this beforehand. Yes, coming to Boston to see Governor Phips had been one reason for the trip, but now she realized that the main reason had been to get her out of Salem. She was angry. Why hadn't he told her this before? She was not a child. But then she looked at her brother. His eyes had welled with tears, his lip was trembling.

"Mary, you must do this. I cannot stand to lose everyone."

In an instant, her anger vanished. She reached across the table and clasped her brother's hand.

He was right. She knew he was right. She would never cry out, but she would not die. She would kill before she would die!

CHAPTER
THIRTY

They brought her through Prison Lane, up Essex Street, then by the First Church and into Town House Lane to the courthouse to be tried.

But a peculiar thing — perhaps befitting the nature of a witch or wizard — was said to have occurred that day as Bridget Bishop passed by the meetinghouse. They said that she paused and looked but briefly toward the house, and immediately a devil flew out from her cap and tore the clapboards down from the northeast corner of the building.

Even stranger, it was reported that some of those same clapboards which had been torn away had, within seconds, been transported to another corner of the building and found to be firmly nailed.

This was Bridget Bishop's last act of witchcraft.

In the first session of the Court of Oyer and Terminer that met on the second day of June, there was plenty to tell of the past sorceries of Bridget Bishop. She had appeared hovering over the bed of one John Cook, grinning evilly, and later that day she caused an apple to fly out of his hands and land in his mother's lap.

John Bly and his wife Rebecca had quarreled with Bridget Bishop over a pig. The pig she had sold them then immediately began to act strangely and was seized with fits. The animal appeared blind and deaf and would not eat or let her piglets suck. Instead, it foamed at the mouth.

William Stacey accused her of causing his cart to lose a wheel in a hole, but when he later went back to look at the hole, the hole was gone. On another occasion, while Stacey was on his way to the brick kiln, Bridget Bishop had flung a curse upon his cart and horse, causing all the gears and tackling to fly apart.

The afflicted girls sat in the front of the court, facing the seven members appointed by William Stoughton, who was the chief councillor himself. Mary Warren, now restored to the ranks of the afflicted, took her place between Ann Putnam junior and Susannah Sheldon. When Susannah was called to testify, she swore that she had seen Bridget Bishop give suck to her familiar, a snake.

One by one, the accusers came forth to list the vile deeds of Bridget Bishop. But most damning of all were the horrid little poppets — dolls, with pins stuck in them — that had been found in Bridget Bishop's cellar. Upon this evidence, Bridget Bishop was condemned to die.

She did, eight days later, at Gallows Hill in Salem where she was hung. The afflicted girls attended the hanging and sat stonily as they watched her body swing from the tree.

"What's that?" whispered Ann Putnam junior. As the noose had tightened, the woman's sphincter had released, emptying her bowels. Little Ann saw the dark fluid stream from under the skirts of the hanging woman, dripping onto the grass below.

"It's the witch bile," replied her mother.

The court worked with great efficiency. On June 29 and 30, Rebecca Nurse, Susanna Martin, Sarah Wildes, Sarah Good, and Elizabeth Howe were tried and condemned to die on July 19.

At some point, toward the end of June, one of the court members — Nathaniel Saltonstall — began to have doubts, most especially about the use of spectral evidence. He resigned his position, but it did not slow down the proceedings.

"Liar! Liar!" Sarah Good had screamed at the Reverend Noyes as the hangman slipped the rope around her neck. "I am no more a witch than you are a wizard. If you take my life away, God will give you blood to drink."

"Reverend, Sir," wrote the Reverend Cotton Mather to his cousin John, "our good God is working of miracles. Five witches were lately executed, impudently demanding of God a miraculous vindication of their innocency. . . ."

The Reverend Mather was reporting the hangings of Rebecca Nurse, Susanna Martin, Sarah Wildes, Sarah Good, and Elizabeth Howe. It was the first mass execution of witches.

It was forbidden that the bodies of witches be buried. So they were thrust into shallow graves in a crevice at the bottom of Gallows Hill. Later that night, however, Caleb returned with the sons of Rebecca Nurse to collect the old woman's body and bury it deep in a wooded place where no one would find it.

The moonlight barely penetrated the thick woods, but the men's eyes had become accustomed to the darkness. Caleb could see that Samuel Nurse's square jaw was slick with tears as he recited the words of the psalm.

"The Lord is my shepherd; I shall not want.

"He maketh me to lie down in green pastures: he leadeth me beside still waters. . . ."

Samuel's voice did not crack. The words flowed steadily.

Caleb could not help imagining himself standing here like Samuel Nurse, perhaps a few short weeks from now. His mother's trial was scheduled for early September. It could not be. It simply could not be!

He looked at the earth where they had just buried Rebecca. The mound of the grave barely showed. They had carefully replaced the moss. No one would find her. It would be some peace of mind to her children that she was not left in that outcropping of granite and felsite to be discovered and pecked by turkey vultures. Samuel now finished reading the psalm. Caleb reached in his pocket.

"Here, Samuel."

"What is this, Caleb?"

"A cross. I made it for your mother."

It was small and carved from teak, its edges beveled and smoothly worked. There were no markings on it.

"But Caleb," Samuel began.

"I know. She was excommunicated, and if they find this cross — but you see, Samuel — " Caleb took the cross and twisted it slightly. The cross immediately came apart in his hand, not into two simple pieces, but into four.

Samuel and his brothers crowded around and stared at the four perfectly crafted pieces of wood.

"Remarkable," said one.

"It is a puzzle."

"Exactly," replied Caleb. "There was a sailor once who came in aboard a ship from far, far away. He showed me something called a Chinese puzzle; it was much more complicated than this, but when you assembled the pieces, they locked together into a six-pointed star. I studied it and figured out how.

These are called cheater dovetail joints," Caleb said, pointing to where the pieces interlocked. "But you see, they work." Quickly he reassembled the pieces into the cross. Then, once more, he took it apart. "Bury these pieces with your mother. No one will know, even if they find them. And — " Now it was Caleb's voice that cracked. "She, being a true Christian, will reassemble them in heaven."

Samuel seized Caleb and hugged him to his chest. Caleb felt their two hearts beating as one. Then the Nurse children, each taking a part of the cross, bent down in the darkness and slipped the pieces into the dirt, under the coverlet of moss.

CHAPTER
THIRTY-ONE

Virginia Chase's prediction had come true.

John Willard, the very constable who had arrested her, had been hunted down as a wizard. Ever since Virginia had spoken those words to him at the time of her arrest, warning him of his own vulnerability, he had found it more and more difficult to do his job.

While Constable Braybrook and Sheriff Corwin had set out each morning with undiminished fervor in their duties of arresting witches and confiscating property, John had found it less and less to his taste. He did not enjoy seeing the children clinging to their mothers' skirts in dismay; the look of either doubt or panic that swept through a husband's eyes as he contemplated the awful question that perhaps he had shared his bed with a woman belonging to the Devil; the utter grief of a man who knew for certain that although the charge was false, the woman who had shared his life and had borne his children was as sure as dead now.

Willard had declared that he had had enough of

arresting witches. He was promptly accused of acts of wizardry.

He had fled in the early part of May. Mary heard about his escape, and in a strange way she was happy, even if he was the man who had arrested her mother. For this was the first time she had heard of anyone escaping.

Her hopes were quickly dashed, however; Caleb reported that Willard had not run far enough. He had been seized and was in prison awaiting trial. Even so, Mary had become obsessed with the notion of breaking her mother out of prison.

Daniel Andrews was another matter. He had actually been arrested and imprisoned, but somehow, just a few weeks after Willard's attempt, Daniel had managed to escape. Ever since Caleb had told her, this had fascinated Mary. How had he done it?

Each week when Caleb came into The Dolphin, Mary asked eagerly if he had any news of Daniel Andrews.

"I am sure," she said, "he did it by sea. He used his shallop."

"From prison, Mary? How?"

"Well, are you sure he was actually taken all the way to jail?"

"Yes. It was not like Willard, who got away before they came for him."

* * *

Then, a week later, Caleb came with truly exciting news. Philip English and his wife, prominent and wealthy people, had both been accused of witchcraft, and both had escaped.

"And you say it is rumored to have been with the governor's help, Caleb?"

"Yes. His own lieutenant governor, Stoughton, sits as the chief prosecutor of the court of Oyer and Terminer, and it's Phips himself who gives him full rein. He has not interfered one bit with the proceedings, but it is said that he privately smoothed the way for the Englishes.

"But Mary, do not get your hopes up. Remember our meeting with the honorable Sir William? We are not the Englishes — Philip English is one of the most important and richest men of the colony."

Mary's eyes still gleamed. She had no faith that the governor would help them, but she was sure that the Englishes' escape had been made by sea. The governor, being a seafaring man, could have easily arranged it, smoothed the way. What they needed was not the governor, but someone like him, a seafaring man with influence.

Unlike Mary, Caleb had been losing hope with each passing day. He took no solace in the fact that some of the accused had managed to escape. Mary, hidden away in Boston, working in the scullery of The Dolphin, was safe in more ways than one. She did not see the interminable parade of the accused to Gallows Hill.

Ever since Rebecca Nurse's execution, Caleb could not drive the terrible images from his mind.

The hangman and his assistant would sling the bound women over their shoulders like trussed-up bales of hay or corn shucks. Carrying their load, they would ascend a ladder to the higher limbs of the tree; then, without ceremony, they would slip the rope around the woman's head and let her go.

There was never a sound and, trussed up like stuffed sacks, the women seemed more like rag dolls than human beings.

Mary seemed to have more energy, more imagination. Her mind was endlessly working on a plan for escape. But Caleb's mind locked on those terrible stuffed bundles swinging from the tree limbs on Gallows Hill.

Escape for her mother, breaking her out of prison, was all Mary thought about. She was sure they could do it. And it would be done by sea. They would sail out of this big bay of Massachusetts into the broad ocean, and they would cross that ocean and sail to another and then another. They would round capes and horns and slide through channels that led to new seas and continents unseen.

They would forever and a day escape from the terrible girls, the vile ministers, the bloated and evil magistrates and councillors. They would leave behind, once and for all, the devils that raged in Massachusetts.

This was what Mary had been thinking about as she scrubbed the linens on the washboard in the courtyard behind The Dolphin. They had to find someone powerful who could help them, a powerful seafaring man. She had been thinking about it for days now.

Her mother's trial was less than two weeks away. It had been hot and muggy. The stench in the North End of Boston was particularly bad when the wind blew humid and warm from the southeast. By all rights, she should be exhausted and cranky like Mrs. Pelham, but Mary had a feeling today, a feeling that something might happen.

She had just hung up the linens and was coming in through the scullery to start up the stew — a hot, onerous task on a day like this. She'd much prefer to be cleaning the fish. Even if it were messy, fish cleaning was cooler. Suddenly Mrs. Pelham came bustling in.

"Mary!" she snapped, but there was no anger in her voice. "I'll do the stew. You clean the fish!"

Mary's eyes flew open in surprise. How could Mrs. Pelham have known her thoughts?

"Sarah," Mrs. Pelham called to the other girl

who worked at The Dophin. "Save that next tub of laundry water. I'll be taking a bath after I get the stew going."

"He must be coming," Sarah whispered. "She ain't never this cheerful, and she never lets anyone else clean the fish 'cept when he come."

"Who?" whispered Mary.

"Captain Coatsworth."

But Mary would always call him the Raven. For with his sharp, dark looks, he bore somewhat of a resemblance to the name of the ship he commanded. The minute he walked through the doors of The Dolphin, Mary knew he was the man who could help them. Of course, getting near him was something else. Mrs. Pelham practically swooned every time he came in during those two weeks. She insisted on serving him herself.

"He is the finest gentleman ever to grace The Dolphin," she sputtered excitedly in the kitchen. "It's been a year since I last saw him. I was worried to death he had perished off Africa with one of them hurricanes or typhoons." She was busy preparing the captain's trencher herself that first evening. "Except for my dear late husband, Diligence Pelham, I never know'd a finer man." She set down the trencher and plucked a handkerchief from her bosom, blew her nose, and wiped her eyes. Then she picked up the tray and went out to serve the captain.

Sarah, a big, rawboned girl from the Cape, snorted. "She does that thing with her hankie every time she mentions her husband in front of us. Just to fool us, you know."

"Why?" asked Mary, peeking out around the door. Her eyes followed Mrs. Pelham as she fairly bounced over to the captain and slid into the booth beside him.

"Why? 'Cause she wants us to think that she still sheds a tear for her husband even though she's going to shed something else for the captain."

"What?" Mary was confused.

"Oh, girl!" exclaimed Sarah. "Never mind. Help me get these trenchers out there. And those rowdies in the corner need more ale."

Mrs. Pelham stayed in the booth all evening with the captain. She grew more and more tipsy, and soon Mary was having to bring them their rum and their pudding. But the captain remained quite sober and attentive, even when Mrs. Pelham became a bit blubbery about her dear late husband. Mary was setting down the pudding when Mrs. Pelham first started to cry.

"Oh dear," Mrs. Pelham said in a tiny, squeezed voice. She must not have realized Mary was right there with the pudding, for she reached into her bodice for her hankie. Then she stretched a bit. Mary nearly dropped the pudding. Half of Mrs. Pelham's immense bosom popped out of the bodice.

217

And although Mary was looking at the bosom, she did not realize that the Raven was instead looking at her, thinking that she was a lovely child; he saw she was spirited, but there was also a sadness about her that disturbed him. He nearly laughed, though, when he saw the shock in the young girl's eyes as she spied Lucy Pelham's breast. This routine of Lucy's was becoming tedious, but she was a sweet old dear.

Mary went back into the kitchen.

The Raven followed her with his eyes. "Tell me, Lucy, dear," he said, turning his attention. "Who is the young serving girl? She's new since I was last here."

"Oh, Mary — she is from Salem Village. A good child and a hard worker. Poor thing. They got her mother in prison for witchcraft." Mrs. Pelham slapped her hand over her mouth. "Oh dear, I wasn't supposed to tell that. Jeremy will have my hide."

"Jeremy? Your uncle up at the Storey Yard?"

"Yes. You see, the girl's brother is apprenticed to him, and you know about all that madness going on up there. Well, you know, we had our own little piece of it down here a few years ago. But this is most horrid, and they got everyone in prison. The prisons are likely to overflow now, and this girl, what with her mother in prison, why they might come after her. So you must keep it quiet, dear." She reached over and touched the captain's hand.

"Of course. You say her brother is apprenticed to Jeremy? Is his name Caleb?"

"Yes, that is the boy."

"He is a fine young carpenter. He did all the scarfing on our torn keel. It was as good a piece of work as a master's who'd been at it for twenty years. And he was only fourteen at the time, I'd wager. So what is her name?"

"Mary. Mary Chase."

Captain Coatsworth couldn't sleep, and it wasn't for the loud snoring of Lucy Pelham beside him. He watched as her pink, fleshy haunches rose and fell, not unlike swells in a windless sea. He liked Lucy a lot. He admired how she had run The Dolphin so well since her husband's death, and although she was a lusty woman, there had never been a breath of scandal about her before Diligence had died. But the empty bed of widowhood was no good for Lucy Pelham. After the hard bunk of the *Raven*, it felt so lovely to sleep beside her. But now, even her softness could not lull him.

He had heard in Liverpool about the troubles in Massachusetts. The Crown never should have appointed that fool, Phips. Meanwhile, the Mathers had wheedled their way into the innermost sanctums, and they had caught the ears of those closest to the new king and queen. But this theocracy had to end.

And the captain could not drive from his mind's

eye the sweet, sad visage of little Mary Chase. Her eyes were too old for her face. Imagine, he thought to himself, enduring a mother imprisoned. And in irons, now that Phips had ordered it for witchcraft. "Irons!" he muttered to the ceiling.

Lucy Pelham coughed, sighed, and turned over, exposing a lovely thigh.

For three nights, the captain couldn't sleep. On the fourth night, he got up and walked to the window of the room and looked out.

Over the rooftops he could see Copp's Hill. The town seemed to grow each time he came back. More ships, more merchants. Even though Phips had driven Massachusetts into debt three years earlier with his exploits in Canada, the town was still growing. It would prosper. Shipping was going to flourish.

New mills had opened right here in the North End. A chocolate mill had just been built on the wharves for processing the cocoa brought into Boston from South America. Warehouses had been built for pickling and drying codfish and shad, which were fast becoming major exports. Shipbuilding was thriving, for there was money to be made in carrying dried fish, and tobacco from the south, and salt pork and grain and apples.

Captain Coatsworth leaned on the windowsill. He turned his gaze toward Hanover Street and sighed. He could see the rooftop of Cotton

Mather's house. Yes indeed, the days of the theocracy were numbered. It was an indulgence in these times to think that one small group of religious zealots could interpret one single God and make rules for a world on the brink of such prosperity.

From the pulpits, these preachers with their Godliness could no longer hold the attention of men of the world — men of trade, men of the towns of Boston and Salem. But who was paying for all this indulgence? From whom was the price being extracted?

From the women, for the most part.

Those pale flowers of the old Puritan world were being cut down as the colony shifted its gaze from God to the sea. But did there have to be this division? Did it always have to be one way?

Coatsworth feared it would, with the narrow vision of men like Cotton Mather and William Stoughton. Yet their time, he felt, was coming to an end. Saltonstall had already resigned. Samuel Sewall, he had heard, was greatly upset. But would it be soon enough?

He looked straight down into the courtyard. Evidently someone else couldn't sleep, either. There was a small figure sitting quietly on the edge of one of the laundry tubs. And she was crying.

CHAPTER
THIRTY-TWO

A fresh breeze blew in from the sea, and of the five witches in the cart being driven through the streets of Salem, one stood erect and proud.

Short in stature, but of great musculature, the Reverend George Burroughs cut an imposing figure even as he rode to his death. The wind ruffled his jet-black hair.

Mary Chase stood in the spreading shadows of the trees at the base of Gallows Hill. She prayed no one would recognize her, but she must find her brother. He had not been at the shipyard, and she was too frightened to ask his whereabouts. But it seemed that he might be here at this dreadful event, for many of the shops were closed, and commerce had ceased.

This was to be a special execution. For George Burroughs was a unique man, and Cotton Mather himself had agreed to travel from Boston for this execution. According to the testimony of the afflicted girls, the Reverend Burroughs was a conjurer above the ordinary ranks of witches. Of all the witches who had been executed, he was the most powerful agent from the invisible world. It was essential that Mather be here. The account he was now writing and planning to rush into print, *The Wonders of the Invisible World*, would not be complete without this event. And Phips had demanded a complete report for the king.

But the events were not unfolding according to plan.

Burroughs was now speaking from the platform. A hush had fallen upon the crowd, and in his deep, thoughtful voice, he spoke so simply and so directly from the heart that the eyes of several in the crowd had begun to brim with tears. There was a rustle and then a whisper as he finished. But he paused only for a moment, and then he began to recite the Lord's Prayer.

"Our Father which art in heaven . . ."

A woman near Mary whispered, "It sounds like the voice of an angel."

This, in fact, was considered to be the supreme test of a witch's guilt. One could not be guilty and recite the Lord's Prayer flawlessly, without a single mistake. But George Burroughs appeared to be doing just that. A murmur swept through the people as he finished.

"Cut him down," yelled a man.

"Yes, cut him down!"

The crowd's frustration was palpable. Cotton

Mather and William Stoughton exchanged nervous glances.

"But I see the Tall Man on his shoulder!" came the piercing cry of Susannah Sheldon, and then the shriller voice of Ann Putnam junior. "Yes, the Tall Man was right there on his shoulder, whispering the words in his ear."

But the crowd was not heeding the girls. They began to press forward toward the ladder. Mary held her breath. Was it possible? Would it all stop now?

Then Mather, still on his horse, rose high in his stirrups.

"Beware! Beware! Be not fooled by this man. The Devil is never more devious than when he appears as the angel of light. Yea, I myself thought I had heard an angel. This man is not what he appears to be."

The mutterings began to subside. Then, in a split second, something happened. A dark blur appeared amidst the branches, as if a very large bird had suddenly crashed. Mary gasped. Something awful was twitching and dangling from the end of the rope. George Burroughs had been hung before the protesting voices had quieted.

The minister from Maine was soon cut down, and his body was dragged to the escarpment, where his trousers were torn from him, and he was shoved into a stony pit.

Mary saw it all.

She ran into a thicket and began to vomit violently. She was so weak from retching that she was forced to lie down for several minutes. But she knew she must get up. She must find Caleb and tell him the plan. There was not a moment to lose.

Later that evening, Caleb returned to the shed where he had been working on the spars of a lighter with another apprentice. The other boy, Joshua, had left to go to the tool room, or so Caleb thought when he was startled by a sound. It seemed to come from a barrel, so it could hardly be Joshua. It must be just a rat, scurrying. But then he heard it again, and his name, too.

"Psst! Caleb!"

No rat had ever called him by name. He saw a cap poking over the rim.

"Mary! What are you doing here? You're not supposed to be here. Joshua will be back any second, and I don't trust him at all."

No sooner had he spoken than footsteps were heard, and Joshua did indeed return. Caleb thought quickly. "I'm going to roll this barrel into Master Jeremy's shed, Joshua. He asked me to do it yesterday, and I forgot. You go ahead with the sanding there."

Joshua nodded. He was just a first-year apprentice, and Caleb was starting his third — so Joshua had to do what Caleb ordered.

Mary felt herself being turned over and then rolled. She had to brace her knees against the barrel's sides to keep from knocking about. She actually began to enjoy it as Caleb rolled her along through the cavernous shed. The world began to capsize in slow rotations as hulls and spars, ribs and keels, turned up, then down, and round and round.

"Now out with it! What is this all about?" Caleb hissed. "You are not supposed to be here. I knew you couldn't stay away from Mother's trial. She thinks we have both left. What if she sees us there tomorrow? It will upset her."

"Be quiet, Caleb."

He was taken aback. His little sister had never spoken to him this way. And it was not impudence. It was a voice as commanding as any ship's captain.

"I have found someone to help us."

"What?" Caleb's heart beat wildly. He blinked. Had he heard her correctly?

"Listen carefully. His name is Captain Eli Coatsworth."

"Of the *Raven*?"

"Yes, of the *Raven*. He comes to The Dolphin. He shares the mistress's bed. He will help us."

"Why?"

226

* * *

The question stunned Mary. Never before had she thought about why Coatsworth would help them. When he had come down and found her that night weeping on the washtub, he had not said why. She had never questioned him. Mrs. Pelham had told him about her mother and why Mary was there. He had merely said, "It's a terrible thing, this Salem business. It must stop. I cannot stop it, but perhaps I can help you."

Mary started to tell Caleb that the reason the Captain was helping them was because he thought this witch business was a terrible thing. But many thought it was a terrible thing — Israel Porter had thought it a terrible thing, even Governor Phips had, for it interfered with his plans to fight Indians, but no one had offered to stop it, or to really help Mary and Caleb.

"I think it is because Captain Coatsworth is a true gentleman, a seafaring man with a good heart," Mary said simply. "Now here is the plan. . . ."

It was a simple plan in many ways. Serving aboard the *Raven* was a master blacksmith whose work was much desired whenever they were in any port. More than once he had made chains and installed iron rings in prisons, although this was hardly his favorite activity. However, Ruben Fifield was devoted to his captain and would do anything Coatsworth wanted. He was also of quick wit and not beyond pulling off a scheme or prank every now and then.

The blacksmith was just one part of the plan. Within a town like Boston, one could find men and women of many talents. Mrs. Pelham knew an artistic young woman who was rumored to be much skilled at calligraphy. Given the proper materials, she could copy anything. In his ship's papers, Coatsworth had some old documents used for customs officers, and various orders from the king or councillors of the colony. Seals could be removed with steam, titles could be copied as well as signatures. It would not take much to fix up a piece of parchment to appear official.

Wave such a document in front of a clerk, claim that orders had been given for the installation of more restraining devices from the governor himself, and Ruben would be inside the prison with his tools in no time. Then it was only a matter of pretending to install a ring or whatever near Virginia Chase.

A few thwacks, and her chains would be severed. The large burlap bag he would bring in with his tools and new chains was of a size to accommodate a full-grown prisoner. And if all that failed, if a guard discovered what Ruben was actually doing, in his pocket he carried ten gold pieces that would prove irresistible to any guard and guarantee his silence.

Caleb shut his eyes. Dare he appear excited? Dare he even hope? But the plan sounded nearly infallible. Could they dream of their mother's freedom? Her trial was to begin the next day.

CHAPTER
THIRTY-THREE

"And you say that Goody Chase came to you?"

"Yes." Ann Putnam junior nodded as did Mary Walcott.

"And what did she say to you?" Magistrate Hathorne asked.

"It was not what she said." Ann Putnam spoke primly. Her mother, who sat a few feet across from where Ann was in the witness stand, lifted her chin slightly and caught the child's eye. "It was what she did," Ann junior added softly.

"And what was that?"

"She bit me." Ann's eyes shifted nervously. "She bit me long." A murmur spread through the courtroom. "She drank the blood from here — " Ann pointed to her chest, "and then she offered it to others, the same way the ministers do!"

William Stoughton leaned forward and whispered hoarsely. "As a black sacrament?"

"Yes." Ann Putnam nodded.

"It's a lie! A damnable lie." Virginia's voice seared the air. "Her mother has put her up to it!"

"Hold your tongue, Goody Chase!" William Stoughton barked.

Ann Putnam's face twisted grimly.

"No, I shall not hold my tongue! It's only a devil of a woman who would put such words in her child's mouth. She has soaked the child in her own bitterness. Painted her mind's eye and imagination in the blood of her miscarried babies. And you, too, Thomas Putnam, it's easier to let your wife rail on this way than to endure alone, day in and day out, her sullenness, her despair. But you are no stranger to bitterness, are you Thomas? It was not a miscarriage that caused your sorrow. No, it was a birth."

The audience stirred. There was not a person who did not know that Thomas Putnam's half-brother, Joseph, had inherited more than was considered his fair share of their father's estate.

Other witches had denied the charges before and called their accusers liars, but none had described in such vivid terms the ones who accused them and their motives. And the picture that Virginia etched in the mind of the jury and the audience was a disturbing one, disturbing because there was in it the ache of their common experience. Every woman in the court that day who had ever miscarried a baby, every family who had ever endured losses, recognized the portrait of bitterness Virginia had drawn.

Everything had been turned topsy-turvy in the

world of Salem Village and Salem Town, Massachusetts. What was bitter now became sweet, and what was loathsome had become alluring. The witch within became the witch outside, and the people could not resist pointing their fingers and crying out. Their souls had become addicted to destroying, and they were more intent and obsessed with this destruction than the angel thrown from heaven, Lucifer himself.

"It's true, is it not?" Virginia wheeled around and pointed her finger at Ann Putnam senior. At just that instant, Ann's hands gripped her neck and she began choking. Then Mary Walcott fell from her seat, choking as well.

"She is choking my mother! She is choking her. Tell her to stop! Tell her to stop," cried young Ann Putnam.

There was great confusion as the girls fell to the floor one by one. Magistrates Corwin and Hathorne raced from their seats.

"We must lead the witch to them so she can touch them, so the evil spirit will flow back into the witch."

"So I am already condemned," Virginia whispered quietly, to no one. "Then let me truly hurt them!"

They led Virginia to Ann Putnam senior, who writhed on the floor. Magistrate Hathorne guided Virginia's hand toward the woman's face.

Suddenly there was a terrible screech as Ann

Putnam's hands flew from the grip around her own neck. Her cheek was streaked with blood where Virginia's nails had clawed the skin.

People crowded about. It had happened so fast that no one was sure what had actually transpired, but Ann Putnam sat still and wild-eyed, touching her cheek. She was not choking. She herself seemed unsure as to what had just occurred. The poison had certainly not flown back into the witch, but in some sort of bizarre defiance, the scientific laws of witchcraft had seemed to reverse.

The others were still choking on the floor. The magistrate did not know what to do. Mary Walcott and Elizabeth Hubbard were nearly blue. So he continued and guided Virginia's hand to Mary Walcott. Once more, a pale cheek was raked in blood. It was the same with Elizabeth Hubbard.

But then, miraculously, the other girls recovered without the touch. The malefic spirit seemed to have automatically flown back into the witch as one by one the remaining girls saw the others' faces streaked with blood.

It did not take the jury long to condemn Virginia Chase of witchcraft. She was, as the law directed, "to be hung by the neck until death on Gallows Hill, two weeks hence on the day of Our Lord October 10, 1692."

CHAPTER
THIRTY-FOUR

Mary Herrick had just finished milking the cows. It was late afternoon. She had poured the milk pans into the bigger buckets. All day, she had been trying not to think about what tomorrow would bring.

Until recently, she had not paid much heed to the goings-on in Salem Town. She barely knew any of the girls except for Mary Warren, who had sometimes come up to Wenham on an errand for her master. It all seemed quite far away, and those girls seemed so different from herself. But it was hard now to stop thinking about it, "the trouble," as her mother called the goings-on in Salem.

It was as if the act of mentioning the word itself was to somehow let the affliction loose, and until they had arrested Mary Esty, it had seemed as if the trouble would never touch them. But Mary Esty had been arrested shortly after the arrest of her sister, Rebecca Nurse. It was Mary Warren herself, along with Susannah Sheldon and Ann Putnam junior, who had given testimony against the old woman.

Tomorrow she was scheduled to die. Mary Esty, who had lived not far down the road from them all of Mary Herrick's life. Mary Esty, who had made bird figures from maple sugar, who had let her ride a pony and had given her a newborn kitten when her old pussy had died. Now Mary Esty was going to die, was going to be hung by her neck on Gallows Hill tomorrow, on the twenty-second day of September. Every time she thought of the rope, the masked hangman, and frail Mary Esty, a hot fearful feeling crept through her gut until her stomach began to churn. How could all this be happening? How could a witch be shaped like Mary Esty? They said the Devil made it so, but how had God let it happen?

Mary Herrick had just hung up the last of the freshly rinsed milking pans when she felt a sudden cool breeze blow through the barn. The pale lavender light of the late afternoon sun turned a bloody red on the horizon. Within seconds, the barn had darkened. Deep shadows crowded in the corners. The chickens stopped their clucking, and the cows in the stalls stopped chewing. An unearthly silence enveloped the barn.

Mary felt her skin prickle and turn cold. She did not want to look, but her eyes were inexorably drawn toward a window high in the hayloft. There, framed by the window and limned by the blood-tinged light of the sun, was the shape of Mary Esty. She smiled down at the girl.

"Tomorrow I am going upon the ladder to be hung for a witch, but I am innocent. And before a twelfth-month has passed you shall believe it."

Mary Herrick told no one of what she had seen in the barn that late afternoon of September 21. On September 22, Mary Esty, Martha Cory, and six others were hung by their necks on Gallows Hill. On the morning of September 23, Mary Herrick began crying out in her sleep. When her parents came into her bedroom, she was doubled over with unimaginable pain. Soon the pain subsided. But the next evening, it returned even worse.

On the third evening, as Mary felt the first terrible stitches deep in her stomach, a cool breeze blew across her cheek. Looking toward the window, she expected to see the shape of Mary Esty's ghost. But it was not Mary Esty whose face loomed on the other side of the window.

"Goody Hale!" gasped the pain-racked girl.

When her parents came into the room, they found the girl worse than ever. She was mouthing gibberish, and her eyes rolled back in her head. She remained in this state for several hours. By morning, the pain had left, but the apparition had not. Still, the sallow, pious face of the Reverend Hale's wife floated in the window, and now she was not alone. For standing inside the window, with a small smile on her face, was Goody Esty.

"Do you think I am a witch?" asked Goody Hale through the window. And then Mary Esty turned to the girl, who lay rigid in the bed, and smiled, as if to say the girl must answer.

"No!" shouted Mary Herrick to the face that floated through the glass of the window. "You are the Devil!"

Then Mary Esty flew beside the girl's bed. Hovering near the bedpost, she spoke. "You see, my dear child, I have been put to death wrongfully and was innocent of the witchcraft. I come" — and her voice sounded as sweet as a bird's song in May — "for vengeance."

With that, she reached over and stroked Mary's brow with cool, transparent fingers. All the pain washed from the girl's body. "For vengeance," Goody Esty repeated. And never had the word been uttered so gently.

CHAPTER
THIRTY-FIVE

C aptain Eli Coatsworth paced in his cabin. He had dreaded this moment ever since he had heard the news from Ruben. The children would be aboard momentarily. They would be expecting to see their mother sitting here in his cabin. They would expect to be hoisting sail for Barbados, and by the time the moon rose, to be on a course out of Massachusetts Bay.

His only hope now was this: Perhaps after the talk surrounding the Reverend Hale's wife, the tide was beginning to turn.

There had been rumors since the end of September of meetings in Boston and Cambridge with ministers in attendance from as far away as New York. It had been said that the Reverend Cotton Mather's father, Increase, the president of Harvard College, had cautioned his son. But it was also true that the book his son was writing defending and explaining the trials was being rushed into print. It was hard to know what to believe anymore.

The mood, however, had changed. Something was different, ever since that child from Wenham had spoken about the ghost of one of the good women executed. Soon after that, the crying out on the esteemed Reverend Hale's wife had begun.

It was shocking, for the Reverend Hale had been one of the most energetic and aggressive of the prosecutors. Now, for him to hear the whispers about the specter of his own wife — the woman who had slept by his side and borne his children — shook him to the very foundations of his faith.

How could he not know what her specter was doing? He was master of his hearth, a fervent preacher of God's word. This could not have been happening under his own roof. The Reverend Hale, as much as any of the prosecutors, had believed in the validity of spectral evidence, but how could the specters have come to pass through his own family?

It was impossible. He simply did not believe it. There could be no doubt of the absolute innocence and piety of his wife; he knew her too well. And yet he realized that this was no defense; for how many other husbands like himself had tried to defend their wives against the same kind of evidence — specters that, until now, he had supported and whose shadowy truths he had used to condemn?

The people of Beverly were stunned by these revelations about their minister's wife. There was talk that the girls had gone too far when they had cried out against her. That the girls were lying.

And yet for Virginia Chase and several others, the death sentence still stood. She was due to hang in two days, and Captain Eli Coatsworth's plan to rescue her had failed.

"What do you mean, she wasn't there?"

Mary's face was white and trembling. And Caleb's thoughts of the plan's infallibility mocked him now.

"I am so sorry, Mary," the captain said.

Ruben, the blacksmith, spoke in a hoarse voice from a corner of the captain's spacious cabin. "They said the prisons were so crowded, they moved at least half a dozen from the Salem jail out to farmers around the county."

"So she is somewhere here in Essex County," Coatsworth said.

"But they wouldn't tell you where?" Caleb asked.

"No." Ruben shook his head. "Not even with this." He took out a gold piece from his pocket.

"Well, we must find out," Mary said firmly. "Somehow, we must find out."

"How, Mary? How is it possible to find out?" Caleb asked as they walked down the wharf in Salem.

Mary drew her cloak around her more tightly. There was a bite in the air, but it was not merely the cold that made her withdraw into the shadows of her hood. In these past weeks of trying to erase her presence from the life of both Salem Town and Salem Village, Mary had come to feel most comfortable in the half light and the darkness. Until the world was set right again, she could not come out into the light of a natural day. How she yearned for that quiet miracle of normal life. Its memory was like a dream from a distant past — as remote as the farthest star.

In the shadowy perimeters of her existence, Mary began to discover another nature capable of deception and possibly violence. Something had turned in her. The anger had hardened into another thing that was best kept in the penumbra of her soul. Within this soul, she imagined both a moon and a sun; and she knew that a strange eclipse had begun to occur.

"The afflicted girls." She spoke in a barely audible whisper. "They often follow the prisoners' cart to Gallows Hill, do they not?"

"Yes," Caleb replied. He was worried and trying to walk faster. He and Mary should not be seen in Salem Town. Even though she had her cloak wrapped tightly, people would see him and know that the slight figure at his side was his sister.

"Remember when the cart carrying Mary Esty became stuck on the hill, and the girls claimed they had seen the Devil wedging the spokes before they reached the steepest part; that they had seen the

Devil and his familiars near the cart when they had picked up Mary Parker? Mary Parker was one of those who had been taken to a farmer somewhere in Topsfield. So how did the girls know where to go to see these familiars? This was before they were on the main road to Gallows Hill. They must have ridden out there."

"And if they do know, do you think they will tell you?"

"Remember what they said about Mother, what she did in court? How she scratched their faces when they led her over to touch the girls in their fits?"

A look of puzzlement filled Caleb's eyes. "Yes, but what does that have to do with finding out where Mother is?"

Mary stopped in the rutted road leading up from the wharf.

"Caleb," she said, her voice low and rough, hardly recognizable. He peered into the shadow of her hood as if to search out the source of the strange voice. "I will scratch. I will cut. I will stab. I will kill to find out where Mother is and save her. They think they have been tormented. They think they have seen a witch. They have known none until now!"

CHAPTER
THIRTY-SIX

There was not a day to spare, for within forty-eight hours, Virginia Chase would die.

Mary and Caleb began to stalk Ann Putnam junior, for they felt that she, of all of them, would know the whereabouts of their mother. But it was hard, because she was always surrounded by elders and powerful people involved in the trials.

William Stoughton had been seen coming from the Putnam house on two different occasions within the space of a morning. Samuel Parris was often there. And Ann Putnam senior kept the child close to her side. Mary Walcott was constantly at the Putnams', and sometimes Mary Warren was there, too.

Of all the girls, Mary Warren was the one most often alone. So, in the late afternoon, Caleb and Mary Chase gave up on Ann Putnam and began to stalk the movements of Mary Warren.

Mary no longer lived at the Procters' home. The children of the imprisoned parents had gone off to live with various relatives. For the most part, Mary had, in recent weeks, been living at Ingersoll's

Ordinary, where she helped with the cooking and cleaning.

Business had been thriving since the beginning of the trials, and it had gotten even better with the closing of John Procter's tavern. On this particular evening, Mary Warren was on her way to Goody Dawson's to pick up some rounds of headcheese, which Goody Dawson was known for.

There was a lonely place in the road not a quarter mile from Goody Dawson's where the land dipped into a swale, and a brook ran across. At this time of year it was dry, and the crossing was not difficult, but the foliage was still thick in a stand of alder and would hide the children. When Caleb and Mary were certain that this was where Mary Warren was heading, they cut across a field and raced to get to the spot in the road where they could hide until she returned with her headcheese.

Mary Warren was thinking about Nathaniel Ingersoll and how rich he was becoming, as she picked her way across the muddy brook, trying to step on the smoothest and largest stones. How nice life had become! The work was not really that hard, and there were no children to take care of.

Sarah Procter had become impossible in her last week there; Mary had feared for her own safety. She had caught Sarah watching her through narrowed eyes with the meanest look imaginable, and she wondered if that rooster with the broken wing was not possibly Sarah's familiar. She had watched carefully and was tempted to say something to Ann Putnam or Mary Walcott. But then she would have been in a pickle, for Sarah was a strong girl and could be of help. And Mary had needed all the help she could get.

Mary Warren had just reached the other side of the brook when she suddenly felt a powerful smack from behind. Her basket went flying. She felt a rock strike her chin, and her face was shoved into the mud. She screamed, but no sound came out.

Then she saw that it was Mary and Caleb Chase who were shoving her down, and Mary Chase was pushing a handful of dried grass into her mouth so she would not scream out.

Mary Chase's face was filled with wrath, and it was as if Caleb's eyes had turned to stone. A bright sliver of light danced across Mary Warren's eyes. Then she felt it — the unmistakably cold edge of the knife at her throat. That was the last thing she remembered before she passed out.

She did not know how long she had lost consciousness. Perhaps it was only seconds, for she was still in the mud, and Caleb's knee was still jammed into her chest as he pinned her shoulders. She was cold, and the wetness of the creek had seeped through her dress.

"Listen," hissed Mary Chase, and she pressed

the blade against Mary Warren's throat. "You tell us where they keep our mother. You tell us, or I'll slice that lying tongue from your mouth."

Mary Warren's terrified eyes slid toward Caleb.

"I'll do it myself, Mary Warren. You are the worst of the lot because you knew the lies, then chose to tell them twice. You know how it is in prison. You've been there yourself. You have seen the worst, and of your own free will, you have chosen to lie yet again and send others to those jails. If ever there was a devil's familiar, you are the one!

"Now we are going to take this grass from your mouth, and you are not going to scream — else quick I will plunge my own knife into your breast and be done with you. And you will tell us where our mother is, and you will not tell a soul of this deed, or else we will come back for you. Mark my words, Mary Warren, I shall come back for you. But do not think of your death, Mary Warren. Think of your salvation. For although you have sent many to the gallows, perhaps by saving one, God will take mercy on you."

Mary Warren felt the blade press harder on her throat, and the grass was finally pulled from her mouth. At last her heart stilled, and a great freedom stole through her mind. The water from the brook ran around her limbs, and she felt, for the first time, blessed. It was over — the lying, the terrible dreams, the terrible voices that had haunted her for months all vanished.

She spoke calmly. "They took your mother to the Moultons' farm. It's in Wenham, just past the Horse Bridge. She is in a sty out behind the barn."

The Horse Bridge was at the head of the Bass River. All the rivers on that neck of land were tidal. At low tide, they were half dry and unnavigable. The children had little more than twenty-four hours now. That meant only two high tides. They would have to procure a boat of some sort and then alert Captain Coatsworth to be waiting for them in a lighter at the mouth.

Time became a blur for Mary and Caleb. Before they had let Mary Warren go, she had told them one more bit of important information. Goody Dawson and her husband had struck a bargain with Constable Braybrook and had come into possession of Sweet Sass as well as the mare. There was too much land to cover, and too little time to do it on foot. Mary and Caleb's first decision was to take back their own horses. So as soon as they had gone to the *Raven* and told Captain Coatsworth of their plans, they headed back in the direction of the Dawsons' farm.

*   *   *

They waited behind a large rock just outside the barnyard. It was strange to see the familiar figure of Gilly going through the same rituals of evening chores in a different barn, on a different farm. How odd it was that this man who had worshipped their father had finally betrayed them.

They did not know how long they would have to wait. It seemed that Gilly was taking his own sweet time. Mary had grown tired and nearly drifted off to sleep while crouched behind the rock. She felt a nudge in her side.

"Look," whispered Caleb.

Gilly was sitting down on the edge of the watering trough. He had bent over and held his head in his hands. With his shoulders hunched, he began to shake. Tremors seemed to course through his entire body, convulsing it. Then they heard the stifled sobs.

"Stay here," whispered Caleb.

Caleb then stood up and moved out from behind the rock. Mary was too frightened to breathe.

"Jacob!" Gilly croaked.

Caleb had come within five feet of Gilly before the sobbing man looked up. "Jacob, it's you! I knew you would come back."

"No, Gilly. It is Caleb."

"Oh, your boy, Caleb. He is doing a fine job down in the Storey shipyard. Yes. Master Jeremy himself told me. Never seen such a fine carpenter at that age. Yes, but Jacob it's terrible times, and I — or this witch plague, and. . . ."

Then Gilly began to sob again.

Caleb walked over to Gilly and touched his shoulder lightly. "Cry no more, old man. The Lord will forgive you, and so will I. Give us our horses."

Gilly stopped crying and looked up. He blinked. The dim eye brightened with a new clarity.

"Caleb," whispered Gilly.

"Yes, Gilly. We need the horses to save our mother."

"Bless you, boy."

"Gilly!" There was a shrill cry from the barn. "Gilly, who are you talking to out there?"

Mary could not remember how she covered the space from the rock to the barn door. She never remembered jumping over the fence. But she was there, on top of Goody Dawson, and Goody Dawson had not even struggled. She had gone down in a soft heap, her temple striking the edge of the barn door.

Gilly and Caleb were immediately at her side. In the moonlight, a lump could be seen rising on Goody Dawson's temple.

"Is she dead?" Mary asked.

"No, she breathes," Caleb told her. "But we must get out of here."

Goody Dawson's eyes flickered open. She stared right into Mary's face.

"Goody Esty," she whimpered. "Goody Esty come to haunt me."

Mary and Caleb looked at each other in stunned silence.

"Quick," rasped Gilly. He had brought the horses around. "Be on your way. You say she is up at the Moultons' farm, by the Horse Bridge?"

"Yes."

"They keep a shallop down on the sandbank of the river."

"Thank you, old man."

Then, both the children turned to embrace him. And for the first time in weeks, Mary felt the darkness inside her begin to lighten, and the sun within her slowly began to slide past the moon.

CHAPTER
THIRTY-SEVEN

They arrived at the Moulton farm just before sunrise.

So many thoughts had been rushing through their minds. Caleb had brought a few tools. He hoped that the chains used to keep his mother in a sty would be easier to break than those in prison, where they were looped through a ring in the stone floor and wall. And what condition would she be in? Could she still walk?

Mary thought only of getting her mother to the river. Once they were on the water, she knew they would be safe. They would simply dissolve into the water network, the liquid web of rivers and streams that would bring them to the sea. They would be as invisible as the voles and burrowing animals in those tunnels that coursed the fields. She remembered the little vole with his quivering whiskers that she had spotted by the road so many months ago. Yes, she and her family would also vanish, but in the end, they would be saved by the captain. She knew it would work. She just knew it.

* * *

They crept up through a back pasture. A wash of pale pink tinged the horizon.

Riders before the dawn. That was what Jacob Chase had called the first light before the sun began its ascent. Jacob had told his children that this was the strongest light of the new day; although it was pale, it held the promise of life to come and had answered the prayers of the night before. And now the crescent of the sun was visible as the first rays sprayed across the field.

Closer and closer Mary and Caleb crept to the sty. Would they hear their mother breathing, the clank of chains? Would there be some sound of life?

And then they both stood in horror. The creak of the sty door swinging in the wind was like nails being driven into their brains. There was a black, gaping darkness.

"Mother!"

No answer.

"Mother!"

"The constable come this morning to fetch her for the hangman," a small voice behind them said.

Caleb and Mary wheeled around. A child of not more than four or five stood in front of them with her pan of grain for the chickens. "Yes, he left here nearly half an hour ago. They are hanging them witches at ten o'clock sharp, and he had more to fetch."

Their throats went dry. Both Mary and Caleb could see their mother's body twitching on the end of a rope. How could this be?

They rushed for their horses.

From the top of a hillock, Mary and Caleb could see the cart of the constable. The route he followed drew him away from the river, and the tide would be starting to turn soon. This end of the river dried out quickly, and within less than an hour, if they did not catch it, it would become impassable.

"We have to think of something. We have to think of something!"

Mary swept back her cap. She was frantic. This was their last chance. With each turn of the cart's wheels, their mother was brought closer to her death. From this distance, they could barely see her in the cart. "Think of something, Caleb! Think!"

But Caleb's mind, too, seemed locked. The constable was a big, strong man. Tackling Mary Warren or Goody Dawson was one thing, but taking on Constable Dewart was another.

"Constable Dewart — was not he the one to fetch Mary Esty when they took her to Gallows Hill?" Caleb asked. "Yes, he was!" he blurted out, answering his own question.

"So?" Mary asked.

"The talk that has been flying about Mary Esty has been thick and full of wild tales. I heard that some people who have spotted her ghost have said that she has often spoken of Constable Dewart and how he will suffer. Only last week I heard a man talking about how the constable had been suffering gout and has been blaming it on Mary Esty's ghost."

"So? I do not follow. Speak more plainly, Caleb."

"The affliction of the girls has been spreading like wildfire — but this is the affliction of guilt. The people are now frightened because it has gone too far. Good, pious people like Mary Esty, and now the Reverend Hale's wife. They are frightened no longer of the Devil, but of God himself. They see ghosts where there are none. Mary, think back. Gilly himself was so choked by guilt that when I stood plainly in front of him, he thought I was our father come back to take vengeance on him for his betrayal. And look at Goody Dawson. She opened her eyes and did not see you, but the ghost of Mary Esty."

Mary was beginning to understand.

"It would not be hard," Caleb continued, "to convince Constable Dewart that Mary Esty's ghost is at large and pursuing him, would it?"

"But it is nearly broad daylight, Caleb."

"No matter. There are ways."

254

They had brought cider in a skin for their mother, but just before Caleb killed the sheep in the field, they emptied the skin so they could bleed the sheep into it.

The sheep they had slain had been munching grass in a field not far from Two Boulders Crossroads. A signpost stood between two large, light-colored boulders there, pointing in the direction of the Village of Salem. The constable would arrive in another quarter of an hour or less. This gave them barely enough time to do their work — and messy work it was.

First, they strung the signpost with the entrails of the slain animal. Then, dipping their fingers in the blood, they wrote the message:

Dewart — the vengeance is mine!

Mary and Caleb crouched behind the largest of the two boulders and waited for the creak of the wheels of the constable's cart. It was not long in coming.

CHAPTER
THIRTY-EIGHT

Constable Dewart had gotten into the habit of whistling as he drove the cart to collect the witches. He whistled to drive away the silence. It was their silence that grated on him. He could not stand it. He would have preferred it if they had ranted and raved and slung curses the way Sarah Good had done. But that had seemed years ago, though it was only a few months. And many a witch and a wizard he had driven since then.

The silence seemed to have thickened and grown more oppressive over time. This Goody Chase was the worst of all. Dear Lord, he hoped after she was dead she wouldn't cause the ruckus that Mary Esty had. It made him fearsomely nervous, all this talk going on about Mary Esty's ghost. And now they were saying that the ghost had been mentioning his name.

But his own wife said that was stuff and non-sense. He should just do his job. God would reward him for helping to clear the colony of the witches. And some of the rewards had already started to

256

come along. Constable Braybrook had been most generous when they went out on the confiscations. He even told Constable Dewart to take his pick of Mary Parker's prize peahens. That had been right kind of him. Dewart knew that Braybrook himself kept a bit of the pewter on occasion, and he supposed that he might help himself to some, too, when no one was looking.

He stopped his whistling. What in the devil was that ahead on the signpost? Looked most odd. He slapped the reins and leaned forward a bit in his seat as they drew closer.

He squinted. Draped over the post, pink and glistening in the early morning sun like some grotesque lacework, were the guts and sinew of an animal. The constable halted the horse and swallowed. He felt beads of perspiration break out on his forehead. A chill ran up his back.

"Aaaargh!" he screamed as he read the words.

A hooded figure jumped out from behind the boulder, but instead of a human face, the head of a sheep stared out at the constable. And this sheep, with eyes pouring blood and little hooves poking from the sleeves of its cape, began to dance.

The very air rained blood. Constable Dewart's last conscious thought was that this was indeed just like what the Reverend Parris had described when he had read the text on Sunday. For here before him was the Book of Revelation come to life at

Two Boulders. The first beast was like a lion. The second beast was like a calf. And then Constable Dewart's heart stopped forever.

She was not chained, for her poor feet and ankles were too swollen and oozing with poison to take her far. But she forgot her pain, and she forgot her sorrow. She looked instead at her two children, smeared with blood, and she praised God. And she whispered to herself that if she in fact died right here and now in her children's arms, all would be well. For they were hers, and she was theirs, and the terrors of the world would never touch them again. Of this she was sure.

"We must go!" Caleb said. "I fear it is too late already for the tide. We can drive this cart as far as the channel and perhaps there find a boat and get downstream to the *Raven*'s lighter."

CHAPTER
THIRTY-NINE

I t blew hard that night, and the ship's surgeon had a difficult time operating on Virginia Chase. But the one foot had to come off if the woman was to live.

Caleb and Mary remained on deck, lashed by sleet as the icy tendrils of the season's first nor'easter blew down upon them. The captain had warned them that it would be a long, gruesome operation, and he did not want them to hear their mother scream out in pain. But it was very odd. Their mother never screamed throughout the entire excruciating three hours.

Mary and Caleb never asked the surgeon what he did with the severed foot. For the first few days, they often wondered. But soon, with their mother's help, they began to laugh about it. Mary would always remember the first time. Heading southeast, they had just crossed the thirty-seventh degree of latitude, halfway between Boston and Bermuda. They were sitting out on deck under a flawless sky and bright sunshine. The water was an intense blue.

Captain Coatsworth had asked the first mate to heave up a bucket of water.

"Feel this, Mrs. Chase," he said, taking her hand and guiding it into the water.

Mary loved the way the captain called their mother Mrs. Chase instead of Goody. For this was what they called governors' and councillors' wives, and women of considerable rank. You could see it in his eyes that the captain thought Virginia Chase to be a woman of considerable rank. And now, when Mary watched him dipping her mother's hand into the warm Gulf Stream water, she couldn't help but remember the stories of the scene in the courthouse when the magistrate had guided Witch Chase's hand to the cheeks of the girls, so the evil would flow back into her.

But there was no evil in this woman. Virginia threw back her head and laughed softly. Her cap slipped off and her pale red hair blew round her face.

"Ah," she sighed. "It's healing, this water."

"When Surgeon Collier takes off the bandages, we'll bring up a bucket to soak your foot, and then it will heal fast."

"Oh, it will?" She raised an eyebrow, her eyes twinkling. "I thought I left that foot behind in the Massachusetts Bay."

That was the first of the foot jokes. There would be more over the years.

JANUARY 17, 1779
EPILOGUE

"**I** thought," she said, "I left that foot behind in the Massachusetts Bay."

Never being as swift of wit as my dear wife, Virginia, and being so smitten by her regal beauty despite the ravages of her term of imprisonment, I was overcome by embarrassment. But I quickly realized, as did others, that none of us need ever suffer an awkward moment because of my wife's amputation. She set an example for all of us and never let her handicap interfere.

Within months after arriving in Jamaica, where we settled for some years before returning to the colony, Virginia was riding a horse. And soon, with a cane and the aid of an attachment carved in teak by Caleb, she was scurrying about the great house on our plantation. It wasn't but three years later that she was able to give up the cane altogether and walk — even run — when she was chasing our rambunctious baby girl, Rachel.

When we finally moved back to Massachusetts, the cold New England winters often caused pain in her stump, and she would resort to the cane in the dampest and bitterest months of winter. Some restitution was made to the many families who had suffered so horribly during those darkest of days of the colony. Nothing could ever, of course, compensate for the lives of so many good women and men that had been so brutally taken during those months, when the madness had descended on the colony of Massachusetts and within the Village and Town of Salem.

Virginia reclaimed the farm she had lost. I was certainly ready for it. Having spent nearly thirty years at sea, the farmer's life had great appeal for me. We all worked hard to realize the dream of Jacob Chase. And it was realized, in a most prodigious manner.

It is for this reason that I now write these diaries and letters, to be read and preserved through the generations to come of our family, our two families — the Chases and the Coatsworths. For although we have prospered materially, we have, through the Lord, been blessed in ways that cannot be measured and weighed in the countinghouses of Derby Wharf, where so many of our children and grandchildren and great-grandchildren now work.

My beloved Virginia has been gone nearly thirty years now. That leaves myself, Mary, and Caleb as among the few surviving members of this colony who lived during those terrible days.

The Devil was indeed thriving in Massachusetts;

he wore a steeple-crowned hat and carried a Bible. His shame is the shame of New England. He left a stain of blood on the fair colony that was indelible. I intend to write about it, for I might be the only one left who can, even though I enter my ninety-fifth year this month.

Caleb's hands are not for writing, and I fear no longer for shipbuilding, so arthritic they have become. But his mind is keen, and his head, at the age of seventy, is not filled with words but with numbers and calculations and equations; he has become the finest of ship designers. He dreams of hulls that can slice through waters in excess of ten knots. He is, of all the Chases, perhaps the dreamer of the largest dreams.

So with Virginia gone, there is only dear Mary — who never likes to speak of those days — and myself to keep the record. Someone must be a witness. Someone must show the way, so that it will never happen again. As my last duty on Earth, I feel a responsibility to write of those days, of the soreness that afflicted men's and women's hearts; and to tell of this one remarkable family that I was blessed to join.

In a few minutes I shall go down to Caleb's shipyard. He expects me on these summer eves. We recall the good times, for mostly there were good times. And how he does love telling the foot jokes that his mother used to make.

"Did you hear the one, Raven, that mother told

at the time of the investiture of the new governor? When he claimed that the councillors did not have a leg to stand on?"

Mary took off her spectacles and wiped her eyes.

She was about to enter her ninety-ninth year. Had it really been thirty-two years since the Raven had died? And only now she had found the letter.

She had to admit that his courage to write about it put her to shame. Yes, the Raven was right, as he had been so often throughout her life. For so many years she could not speak of it.

Oh yes, she had told her children and her grand-children how Grandma had lost her foot because of the prison irons, and she and her husband, Martin, would patiently explain about the terrible witch trials. But to be honest, she had let her husband do most of the explaining. It had troubled her to speak of it, and it had troubled her not to, as well.

She rubbed her fingers against her temples. But now, of course, Martin was gone. He could no longer do the speaking. She looked down at the desk where she sat. On the drawing board was an old ship design, one that she and Caleb had worked on years before when their yard first began building ships for the China trade. She always enjoyed look-ing at a well-drawn plan for a full-rigged ship. It was as beautiful as any painting or any silver piece.

But perhaps the time had come to make new marks on paper.

Mary Chase Shields reached for the lovely dovetailed box that she had made almost eighty-five years before. She opened its lid with the beveled edges. From it, she picked up a quill pen. Then she closed her eyes and tried to remember back to that winter nearly eighty-seven years before. Yes, it was January, early January, just as it was now. And there was an afternoon, a cold afternoon, with a breeze off the sea.

She looked out the window from her tall brick house on Derby Street. The light was not that different. Light does not change, she thought — but within men's souls, it can. And she began to remember the sun and the moon that she had imagined within her own soul that winter, and the strange eclipse that was about to begin, and the long darkness of her heart.

She dipped the pen in the inkwell and began to write.

AUTHOR'S NOTE

Although *Beyond the Burning Time* is a work of fiction, it is rooted in well-documented American history. As a novelist of historical fiction, I work within a tradition where facts and actual recorded events are used, and on some occasions expanded upon, within what I consider the strictures of logic and judicious imagination.

When I have altered facts in this novel, I have tried to remain faithful to the historical period in which they occurred. My goal is to present young readers with a compelling story that will introduce them to the dynamics of the Salem witch trials, hopefully encouraging them to think about this fascinating but troubling time. It would be a disservice indeed if the essential fabric of the period were torn in the process. I would like to be as clear as possible regarding the sources I have used as the basis for my story, and in which cases I have added fiction to the facts.

At the time of the Salem witch hysteria, the Commonwealth of Massachusetts was without a legal charter, and for much of that time, it was also without a governor.

In 1684, the charter — a document that provided the means whereby courts of law could be convened and land titles could be granted — had been revoked by then-governor Edmund Andros. The people were enraged. Without a charter, their titles to land were jeopardized, and in 1688, they overthrew Andros.

By late 1691, when the hysteria began, there was no basis for a process of legally governing. The Commonwealth was like a ship without a rudder, and the people were thrown into great doubt and confusion.

These conditions of uncertainty, perhaps, helped to lay the groundwork for the deadly events that followed in Salem Village. For it was, in fact, a lawless time, and those bent on destruction could proceed fearlessly without obstruction or interference.

The Chase family and many of the characters in this story, such as Goody Dawson, Benjamin Dawson, Gilly, and Eli Coatsworth, are fictional creations. But many others, such as John Procter, Tituba, Sarah Good, Sarah Osburne, Nathaniel Ingersoll, Samuel Parris, and all of the girls who were the accusers, as well as Ann Putnam senior and her husband, Thomas, were real people who lived and participated in the village life of Salem. Their deeds, and in many cases, their words, were recorded and can be found in several books on the period and documents that are in the archives of the Essex Institute of Salem, Massachusetts.

The testimonies of Sarah Good, Sarah Osburne, and Tituba, found in Chapter Eleven of this book, were excerpted verbatim from the court reports and examinations conducted by John Hathorne and Jonathan Corwin, collected in two volumes of witchcraft papers of the Essex County Archives: *Salem Witchcraft, 1692*, as well as in Charles Upham's account published in 1867.

In Chapter Twenty-one, the excerpts from Deodat Lawson's sermon and the words describing Ann Putnam senior's seizure were excerpted directly from Lawson's work, *The Brief and True Narrative*, published in 1692 and included in *Narratives of the Witchcraft Cases*, edited by George Lincoln Burr. Other direct quotes were the words of Mary Warren when she confessed that the "girls did but dissemble," and that the accusations had been made just "for sport." She spoke these words on separate occasions prior to her arrest in the late spring of 1692.

It is also true that Goodwife Sibley recommended that a witch's cake of rye baked with children's urine and fed to a dog could be used as a method for extracting the names of the girls' tormentors, and Tituba did, in fact, bake that cake. The report of Mary Herrick seeing the ghost of Mary Esty can be found in several historical works and accounts of the times. Also, it should be noted that Sarah Good's prophecy from the gallows that God would give the Reverend Noyes blood to drink if she were hung came true a few months later when the Reverend died of a massive hemorrhage.

It is true that Mary Walcott, Ann Putnam junior, and Mercy Lewis were asked to visit a nearby town to ferret out witches suspected of tormenting people. The town, however, was Andover and not Topsfield, and the event occurred a month later than suggested in this story. The proceedings I described for determining a witch's identity are accurate. This was the first time the blindfold test was used, which gave a new, and even more preposterous twist to the great fabrication of spectral evidence.

I am deeply indebted to the work of Paul Boyer and Stephen Nissenbaum for their documentation of property transactions and tax records, which made it all too clear that old grudges, jealousy, and money had as much to do with the tragedy of Salem as superstitions.

In all, twenty-four people died because of the Salem witch hysteria and trials. Nineteen people were hung, Giles Cory was pressed to death by stones, and the other four people died in jail. In the fall of 1692, Governor Phips' own wife was cried out upon as a witch. It was shortly thereafter, on October 12, that the governor informed the Privy Council in London that he had forbidden further witchcraft imprisonments. On October 29, Phips dissolved the Court of Oyer and Terminer, and in November, the General Court of the colony created the Superior Court to try the remaining witches. Finally, in May 1693, Governor Phips pardoned all those still in prison on charges of witchcraft.

In 1752, Salem Village was separated from the town of Salem and was officially incorporated. At that time the name of the town was changed to Danvers. In 1992, the town of Danvers dedicated a monument to the memory of those who died during the Salem witchcraft hysteria.

Although some of the facts and the spellings of names vary in reference works, few events of three hundred years ago were so completely documented through public records, eyewitness accounts, and personal narratives as the Salem witch hysteria and trials. Despite the overwhelming evidence, there will always be those who say it never happened. The abyss of their ignorance can only be a void to invite more persecution. But to those who are not ignorant, may we all join and say, "never again."

I dedicate this book to the following persons who died in the Salem witch hysteria:

Sarah Osburne, of Salem Village, died in jail May 10
Bridget Bishop, of Salem Village, hung June 10
Unnamed child of Sarah Good, born and died in jail

Sarah Good, of Salem Village, hung July 19
Elizabeth Howe, of Topsfield, hung July 19
Susanna Martin, of Amesbury, hung July 19
Rebecca Nurse, of Salem Village, hung July 19
Sarah Wildes, of Topsfield, hung July 19
The Reverend George Burroughs, of Wells, Maine,
   formerly minister of Salem Village, hung
   August 19
Martha Carrier, of Andover, hung August 19
George Jacobs, of Salem Village, hung August 19
John Procter, of Salem Village, hung August 19
John Willard, of Salem Village, hung August 19
Ann Foster, of Andover, died in jail
Giles Cory, of Salem Village, pressed to death
   September 19
Martha Cory, of Salem Village, hung September 22
Mary Esty, of Topsfield, hung September 22
Alice Parker, of Andover, hung September 22
Mary Parker, of Andover, hung September 22
Wilmot Reed, of Marblehead, hung September 22
Ann Pudeator, of Salem Village, hung September
   22
Margaret Scott, of Rowley, hung September 22
Samuel Wardwell, of Andover, hung September 22
Sarah Dastin, of Reading, died in jail.

KATHRYN LASKY
January 1994
Cambridge, Massachusetts

FOR FURTHER READING

Boyer, Paul and Stephen Nissenbaum. *Salem Possessed: The Social Origins of Witchcraft.* Cambridge: Harvard University Press, 1974.

Burr, George L., ed. *Narratives of the Witchcraft Cases: 1648–1706.* New York: Charles Scribner's Sons, 1914.

Conde, Maryse. *I, Tituba, Black Witch of Salem.* Charlottesville: University Press of Virginia, 1992.

Demos, John. *A Little Commonwealth: Family Life in the Plymouth Colony.* Oxford, England: Oxford University Press, 1970.

Silverman, Kenneth, ed. *Selected Letters of Cotton Mather.* Baton Rouge: Louisiana State University Press, 1971.

Starkey, Marion L. *The Devil in Massachusetts.* New York: Doubleday, 1949.

ABOUT THE AUTHOR

Kathryn Lasky is the author of more than thirty fiction, nonfiction, and picture books for young readers. Her award-winning books include *Sugaring Time*, a Newbery Honor book; *The Night Journey*, winner of the National Jewish Book Award for Children; and *Pageant*, an ALA Notable Book. Ms. Lasky is also a recipient of the prestigious *Washington Post*-Children's Book Guild Award for her contribution to children's nonfiction. She lives in Cambridge, Massachusetts, with her husband, photographer Chris Knight, and their two children.

ALSO BY KATHRYN LASKY

Fiction

The Night Journey
Beyond the Divide
Pageant
The Bone Wars
Jem's Island
Double Trouble Squared
Shadows in the Water
A Voice in the Wind

Nonfiction

Sugaring Time
A Baby for Max
Puppeteer
Dinosaur Dig
Traces of Life
Think Like an Eagle
Surtsey: The Newest Place on Earth
Searching for Laura Ingalls
Monarchs
The Day of the Dead

Picture Books

Sea Swan
Fourth of July Bear
I Have an Aunt on Marlborough Street
The Tantrum
My Island Grandma
The Solo
The Librarian Who Measured the Earth

Beyond the Burning Time was typeset in Times Roman
by N.K. Graphics, Inc., Keene, New Hampshire.
The display type was typeset in Acquitaine Initials.
The book was printed on 55-lb. Renew Antique paper and
printed and bound by Berryville Graphics, Berryville, Virginia.
Production supervision by Michael Roche.